Valentine's Day
Can Be Murder

**Other Books by
Colleen O'Shaughnessy McKenna**

Too Many Murphys

Fourth Grade Is a Jinx

Fifth Grade: Here Comes Trouble

Eenie, Meanie, Murphy, No!

Murphy's Island

Merry Christmas, Miss McConnell!

The Truth About Sixth Grade

Mother Murphy

The Brightest Light

Camp Murphy

Cousins: Not Quite Sisters

Cousins: Stuck in the Middle

Good Grief . . . Third Grade

Live From the Fifth Grade

Dr. Quinn, Medicine Woman: New Friends

Valentine's Day
Can Be Murder

Colleen
O'Shaughnessy McKenna

AN
APPLE
PAPERBACK

SCHOLASTIC INC.
New York Toronto London Auckland Sydney

No part of this publication may be reproduced in whole or in part, or stored in a retrieval system, or transmitted in any form or by any means, electronic, mechanical, photocopying, recording, or otherwise, without written permission of the publisher. For information regarding permission, write to Scholastic Inc., 555 Broadway, New York, NY 10012.

ISBN 0-590-67985-6

12 11 10 9 8 7 6 5 4 3   6 7 8 9/9 0 1/0

Printed in the U.S.A.   40

First Scholastic printing, February 1996

*This book is dedicated with love
to my daughter Laura,
my most special holiday present of all.*

Valentine's Day
Can Be Murder

1

I was in the middle of showing my best friend, Patrick Frank, the Nolan Ryan rookie card I got for Christmas when I was rudely interrupted by the most annoying girl in our fifth-grade class, Marsha Cessano.

"So what *else* did Santa Claus give you, Roger Friday?" she asked. "Or did you just get your annual lump of coal?"

"Well, I didn't get what I *really* asked for," I shot back. "Or you'd be swinging from a vine in Peru right now."

Patrick and Marsha's good friend, Collette, started to laugh. Marsha elbowed Collette.

"Don't laugh at him, Collette," Marsha insisted. "I guess he got a new joke book in his stocking."

"No," I said. "But eleven years ago, the stork left a joke for your parents. And they named her Marsha."

Within seconds, Marsha's nail-bitten fingers were around my neck.

"Take that back!" she sputtered. Up close, Marsha smelled like Froot Loops.

"Hey, psycho-woman," I gasped, prying her suction-cup fingers from my neck. "I was kidding."

Mrs. Pompalini, our fifth-grade teacher, rushed down the aisle. "Marsha, get your hands off Roger this instant!"

I rubbed my neck and then hung my head to one side. With any luck, Marsha would serve the first detention of the new year.

"Honestly," cried Mrs. Pompalini. "You know my rules about respecting one another. Is this any way to start the new year?"

Marsha shook her head, trying to look normal. Not an easy task for this girl.

"Should I go to the nurse, Mrs. Pompalini?" I asked in a weak voice. "Maybe she has some electrical duct tape for my neck."

Mrs. Pompalini grinned. Usually she thinks I'm pretty funny. Except when I put the dead snake in Marsha's locker a few months ago. I ended up with a trillion weeks of detention.

"You seem to be okay," she declared, moving my head up and down. "Will someone explain what happened?"

"It was all my fault," I said quickly. "I made a *huge* mistake."

Marsha's mouth fell open at my easy confession.

"Yeah," I continued. "I got too close to Marsha's cage."

"Very funny," snapped Marsha. "Remind me to laugh." She turned to our teacher. "You should have heard him, Mrs. Pompalini. Roger insulted me, then he insulted my parents. And my mother is homeroom mother!"

Mrs. Pompalini's eyebrows slowly rose. "Well, all parents should be shown respect, Roger."

"Roger was joking," Patrick said quickly.

Collette nodded her head. Collette may be Marsha's neighbor and friend, but she's my friend, too. With two younger brothers, she knows joking is not a big deal.

Luckily the first bell rang, and Mrs. Pompalini headed back to her desk. She turned at the end of the aisle and pointed her finger at me. "You have managed to stay out of trouble ever since the dead snake episode, Roger. Don't spoil your good record."

As soon as Mrs. Pompalini turned her back, Marsha poked me in the side with her finger. "You'll have a *police* record as soon as I tell my mother what you said about the stork!" She licked her fingertips and tried to smash down her bangs. "My aunt is a crossing guard and knows two policemen by their first names!"

"Oh, yeah," I replied. "Well, my uncle runs a doughnut shop near the police station, so he even knows what the whole police force takes in their coffee!"

"Big deal," Marsha muttered as she slumped into the seat behind me.

Mrs. Pompalini flicked the lights on and off. "Take your seats, children. I have some exciting news!"

I sat down. Great! Maybe our gym teacher finally got the new baseball shirts. I wanted thirty-four, Nolan Ryan's number.

"Welcome back, and Happy New Year!" Mrs. Pompalini said. She blew on a yellow party blower and tossed a little confetti up into the air. We all laughed. Mrs. Pompalini was so much fun.

"This year, Valentine's Day will be celebrated with a dance for fifth and sixth graders!"

A girl in the front row clapped, then quickly folded her hands. The rest of the room stayed silent. A dance? Our principal, Sister Mary Elizabeth, usually let only the seventh and eighth graders have dances.

"The money raised will be used to donate Easter baskets to homeless children," Mrs. Pompalini continued.

Patrick raised his hand. "Do we have to go?"

Mrs. Pompalini grinned. "No, but it will be fun! Secondly, there will be a contest for the best valentine box, so bring yours in as soon as possible."

I groaned. Valentine's Day was over a month away. Besides, valentine boxes were dumb! I would skip the dance and the valentine box.

Collette raised her hand. Good! She must think the idea of valentine boxes was silly, too. She is one of the smartest girls in the class, so she would find a polite way to tell Mrs. Pompalini to cancel the corn.

"How soon can we bring the valentine boxes in?" asked Collette.

I let my head thump down on my desk. I would rather do a zillion math problems than this baby stuff.

"All boxes should be on the back radiator by the first week in February," said Mrs. Pompalini.

I raised my head. "Can I keep mine at home? Maybe just leave a forwarding address on the radiator?"

Patrick laughed. Marsha kicked the back of my chair.

"All boxes on the radiator," Mrs. Pompalini repeated. "Especially yours, Roger."

"Even though it will stay empty," Marsha hissed. She's very snakelike at times.

Someone knocked on the door and Mrs. Pompalini held up both hands. "I'll bet this is our second exciting surprise!"

"I hope you ordered double cheese on mine," I called out.

Sister Mary Elizabeth walked in, followed by a girl with thick black hair. She kept her eyes down, like she was nervous. Then, all of a sudden, she looked up at our class and flashed a big smile. That's when her dimples kicked in!

I sat up straighter.

"Class, please welcome Stacy Trinidad from Santa Fe, New Mexico," said Sister.

"Hi," said Stacy, shaking back a yard or two of shiny hair.

"Hi," our class answered back.

"Welcome," I added, my voice cracking.

Marsha kicked the back of my chair again. My first impulse was to reach back and shove my eraser down her sock. My second impulse was to grin at Stacy as Mrs. Pompalini led her to the empty desk beside me.

2

For the next three weeks, I tried to stay out of trouble as much as possible. It wasn't because I finally decided to end my lifetime feud with Marsha; the girl still drove me nuts. But I didn't want Stacy to think I was a jerk. So I kept my wisecracks to Marsha down to two or three a day. During the first week in February, Stacy brought in her valentine box. Later that afternoon, I told Mrs. Pompalini I was going to bring in my valentine box. I figured it would be the only way Stacy would be able to send me a valentine.

I found a great toaster-oven box in our garage as soon as I got home from school on Tuesday. I knocked a few spiderwebs out of it, then grabbed a can of bright red spray paint from the garage and painted it. Once it dried, I spent two hours pasting on every picture of New Mexico I could find. Stacy had told the class that in her old school, they pasted beads on their boxes. I pasted a few pieces of pasta on mine. It looked pretty good. By the time I was finished, the idea of a valentine box wasn't so dumb after all.

The next morning, I walked slowly down to the bus stop, carrying my valentine box. "Where is our bus anyway?" I asked Patrick. "It's late!"

Patrick checked his watch, which tells the time in every country in the world. I was tempted to ask him what time it was in Santa Fe. "The bus is exactly seventeen minutes late. If it doesn't show up soon, we are within our legal rights to go back home." Patrick grinned and crossed his fingers. He's the smartest kid in fifth grade.

I craned my neck down Heberton Avenue, wishing the bus would hurry. As soon as I got to school, I wanted to set my valentine box next to Stacy's. "We're going to be late."

Patrick started to laugh. "Since when did *you* start liking school?"

Since Stacy, I thought. "Who said I did?" Patrick and I had been best friends since kindergarten. We tell each other everything. Well, almost. I still hadn't told Patrick that I liked Stacy. I didn't know if I was embarrassed or afraid Patrick might like her, too. What would I do then? Patrick and I share all the time — our lunches, baseball bats, and last summer at camp even a toothbrush for a week. But I wasn't so sure about sharing a girl. I didn't know why.

But Patrick was my best friend.

When the bus rounded the corner and turned

on its flashing yellow lights, I decided to tell Patrick that I liked Stacy before the homeroom bell rang. Well, maybe that would be rushing it, but I would positively tell him before lunch. Okay, maybe *after* lunch, but absolutely before recess ended. And if recess got too crazy I would definitely tell him all about it on the bus ride home.

"Are you going to give out any valentines this year?" Patrick asked.

"A couple," I said. One for Stacy, one for Mrs. Pompalini. "Do you want me to buy you a box of candy or something?"

Patrick grinned. "Sure! Caramels would be nice." Patrick reached in his backpack and pulled out a stack of white envelopes. "I have twenty-three."

"One for every kid in the class?"

Patrick nodded. "It seems like the fair way to handle it."

"Maybe I should do that, too," I said. "I could always put a few dead flies in Marsha's card. Sign it, 'Love from your trash-can friends'."

When the bus pulled up to the school it started to rain, so Sister opened the double doors and everyone hurried inside.

"What's going on over at the bulletin board?"

About twenty or thirty kids were gathered around the bulletin board outside the principal's office. Everyone was shoving and elbowing each other to get closer. "Maybe Marsha finally hit the FBI's Most Wanted list," I suggested.

Patrick snickered.

The bulletin board is usually pretty dull, holding the names of kids with overdue library books, or flyers about skating parties. Today's news had to be different. Patrick and I wormed our way over. In the center of the board was a large red heart. In black Magic Marker was the word DANCE.

"Oh, great. I had forgotten about the dance." A dance notice was a lot more threatening than an overdue-library-book notice. The only thing a librarian could do was yell at you and make you pay a lot of money. Going to a dance was more dangerous. At a dance you could make a total fool of yourself in front of the *whole school*. Then Marsha would spend the next ten years reminding me of how I made a real jerk of myself. She would probably announce it at our high school graduation. I'd give Stacy a valentine, and maybe even sign my name. But there was no way I would go to the dance on Friday.

3

"**A** dance!" Patrick laughed, turning away from the bulletin board. "Like we care!"

"Yeah," I added, trying to laugh myself. "Like either one of us knows *how* to dance."

Patrick scratched his chin. "I hope Mrs. Pompalini isn't giving extra credit for attending. I just don't *want* to dance."

"Let's go to homeroom," I suggested, gesturing with my valentine box. "I want to put this on the radiator with the others." My box didn't look as fresh as it had when I left my house. Some of the pictures were already curling at the ends like my dog's tongue on a hot day. Two of my pasta shells were missing.

"Patrick, how does this box look to you?" I asked.

"*Lovely! It's a dreamy box!*" Marsha Cessano burst out of nowhere to tap on the side of my box. "Is it ticking? Or are you just trying to smuggle in another dead animal, *Mr. Road-kill?*"

My eyes shrank to near-slits. That voice. Those shrieky syllables held together with a thin nasal whine.

Marsha! I couldn't look. That girl in full throttle is not a pretty sight.

Patrick and I accelerated, but Marsha shifted gears and caught up. She elbowed me and smiled. It was not a *nice* smile; it was the kind villains and monsters flash in comic books.

"I saw you looking at the dance poster," Marsha said. "If I were you, I'd forget about going to the dance. Ask your mom to take you to Chuck E. Cheese for pizza. If you eat all your crust, they'll give you a free balloon."

"Maybe we *should*," Patrick whispered. "Friday's double cheese night."

"Ignore her," I instructed him. We started walking faster.

"Oh, don't go away *mad*," called Marsha. "Just go away."

I saw Stacy standing by her locker. Fate was trying hard to bring the two of us together. First she got the desk next to mine, then Collette offered to share her locker with Stacy. Collette's locker is right next to mine.

"Hi," Stacy said.

"Hi," I said.

"Morning," Patrick muttered as he rushed by to his locker. Patrick was still more comfortable around math problems than around girls.

"Are you going to the dance?" Stacy asked.

"Maybe," I said quickly. My ears zapped red, my mouth became dry. Why couldn't I grin and say, "Speaking of the dance, Stacy, I'll meet you in the school gym at seven and we can dance the night away." Then I would wink, maybe twice. Switch eyes or something.

"Are you okay, Rog?" asked Stacy. "Is something in your eye?"

I shook my head, turning to shove my entire upper body into my locker. "I'm fine," I croaked.

"I see you brought your valentine box, Roger," she said. "I brought mine in last week."

I glanced into the room, at Stacy's box. It was perfect. Just like Stacy.

"Now I worry if I'll get any valentines," Stacy said slowly. "I mean, not too many people even know me."

"I do!" I wanted to shout. As the morning bell rang, I began to smile, my plan forming. Stacy had no idea anyone liked her. But all that would change when she read the valentine I was going to give her.

My smile grew so broad it slid across my face and around the back of my head. I closed my eyes and pictured Stacy opening her valentine box. I was still smiling when I walked face first into the wall.

4

Stars jitterbugged around me. I tried to smile and pretend that I had *purposely* walked into the wall, but my mouth wouldn't work.

"Roger, are you all right?"

"Use the door next time, Roger," said Marsha as she pushed past me.

"I guess I took a wrong turn," I mumbled, rubbing my jaw.

I felt Stacy's hand on my arm as she walked past. "I am always tripping over something. My mother is forever telling me that I have two left feet."

As soon as Stacy was out of sight, I rubbed my nose and forehead. "Whoa, I think I cracked my brain. My head is killing me!"

Patrick stood in front of me, studying my face. "Your nose looks a little off center, Roger. Maybe you ought to go to the nurse. Or a surgeon."

I groaned. "I can't believe I did that."

The first bell rang as I carried my valentine box

15

to the radiator and then slid into my seat. I couldn't talk to Stacy now. It would just give her a closer look at my off-center nose and cracked forehead.

From my desk I watched Stacy shake her valentine box. Two other boxes and mine were already there. Stacy, Sarah, and Collette were complimenting each other on their decorations.

"Now we just have to wait and see if any valentines go in the boxes," said Stacy.

Collette nodded. "My mom says that the first valentine you receive is always the most special."

I leaned forward. I had never heard that before. It sounded true.

"Collette, I'll save my first valentine this year," confided Stacy. "My first valentine received in Pittsburgh."

I turned around in my seat, ripping a sheet of notebook paper out of my folder so quickly that it tore in half. I tried again, slicing two fingers with the edge of the paper. Blood smeared across the top half. I crumpled both sheets up and tugged at another sheet.

"What are you doing to your notebook, psycho-man?"

I jerked my head up and frowned at Marsha.

"Settle down, Roger," Marsha mumbled as she carefully snapped open my folder and handed me a sheet of paper. "I think you might have blown a fuse when you whacked into that wall. Are you okay?"

"Fine!" I snapped, taking the paper with my fingertips.

Marsha gave me another careful look and walked away. I closed my eyes and drew in a deep breath. All right now, relax, Roger. All you have to do is jot down a quick little verse, draw a red heart around it, and sneak it into Stacy's valentine box while no one is looking. The important thing is to be the very *first* person to give her a valentine.

I hunched over my paper and eyed the rest of the classroom. Had anyone else heard Stacy and Collette talking? Was someone else writing her a valentine?

Except for Larry Bolter, who was trying to dangle a pencil from his left nostril, nobody was even sitting down.

I wiped my bloody finger on the inside of my sock and picked up my pencil. Okay now. Five more minutes before second bell. Then, while everyone was scrambling around getting books out and pencils sharpened, I would race out of my seat, pretend I was looking at the globe, and stick my poem in Stacy's valentine box.

I chewed on the end of my pencil, wondering if I could use a verse from last year. Maybe the one I slipped into Marsha's locker in fourth grade:

ROSES ARE RED.
VIOLETS ARE BLUE.
MY GYM SOCKS SMELL GROSS,
BUT STILL BETTER THAN YOU!

Or I could try the one I snuck into her lunch bag in third grade. I smiled, remembering Marsha's face when she found it taped to her baloney sandwich.

ROSES ARE RED.
VIOLETS ARE BLUE.
MY DOG HAS FLEAS,
WHICH LOOK JUST LIKE YOU!

My smile disappeared as I glanced at the clock. I couldn't use anything insulting. I wanted Stacy to *like* me, not hate me the way Marsha did.

I closed my eyes, tapping my pencil against my blank paper. Stacy was harder to write for. She deserved something nice and friendly. A valentine that mothers and grandmothers would pass around and finally tape to the refrigerator. Cards without insults took more time.

FLOWERS SMELL FRESH AND NEW.
RAINBOWS STAY IN THE SKY WITHOUT
GLUE.

I reread it a couple of times. It wasn't very good. I reached inside my folder and carefully pulled out another sheet of paper. The bell was going to ring any minute. I looked around the room, at the blackboard, the flag, the trash can. The trash can! Joey Morelli pitched a wad of purple gum inside. Thwack! Direct hit. Definite stick.

I bent my head and started printing as fast as I could.

ROSES ARE RED.
VIOLETS ARE BLUE.
GUM STICKS TO METAL
AND I'M STUCK ON YOU!!!!

I reread it, pleased. Not insulting, not too mushy. It was funny, but kind of serious, too. Picking up my red marker, I drew a large heart, then added two little hearts at the bottom. While I was trying to decide how to sign off, the bell rang. I folded the poem; names could come later.

"Let's get settled," Mrs. Pompalini called out, flicking the lights on and off.

I flew out of my seat in a flash. I studied the valentine boxes, then slapped my left hand on top of the globe. I bent down, spinning the globe, while my right hand reached out behind me and stuck the valentine into Stacy's box. I was back in my seat before the globe had even stopped spinning. Mission accomplished.

5

When the bell rang for lunch, an alarm went off inside me. Any minute now Stacy would hurry back and find my valentine. My own stomach rumbled, but I couldn't think about food. I spotted Stacy already in line. I bolted for the line, knowing I had to bring up the subject of valentines quickly and wait for Stacy to check her box.

I snuck in behind her while two kids investigated each other's lunch bags. Stacy was busy talking to Marsha and Collette.

"I am really hungry. I hope we have *valentine* cookies for dessert," I said.

The two boys behind me looked up from their lunch bags. "Hey, how did you get here, Roger?"

"He snuck!" Marsha announced from the head of the line. "No cuts, Friday!"

"Yeah, step to the rear," added one of the kids behind me.

"Settle down, class!" called Mrs. Pompalini.

Stacy turned and smiled at me. "You must be *real* hungry today, Roger."

"Yeah, I am," I said quickly. "I have to keep my energy up for *Val-en-tine's* Day." I hoped a bell would go off in Stacy's head.

"Not too much longer," Stacy agreed.

"The valentine dance will be so cool," Marsha blurted out. "I heard that maybe Sister Mary Elizabeth will let some of the seventh graders come. I mean, only the nice ones who don't get detention."

Stacy and I started laughing.

Marsha looked offended, which is her usual look. "So, what's so funny about that?" She wanted to know. "My father would be very upset if some rude, detention-serving seventh-grade boy tried to dance with me, and . . ."

"And discovered you were an alien?" I asked. The words were out of my mouth before I even knew I was saying them. A bunch of kids laughed. Marsha's face flooded red. Stacy stared at me.

I didn't mean to make fun of Marsha. I mean, I *do* enjoy making fun of her, but not if it bothered Stacy.

"Just kidding, Marsha." Everyone started filing out into the hall. Marsha strutted off in a huff.

"Hey, Stacy, don't take all this the wrong way," I wanted to say. "Marsha and I enjoy insulting each other. It helps our blood circulate. It keeps our brains in tip-top shape."

21

Hard as it was to do, I kept my mouth shut. I didn't say a word all the way down to the cafeteria.

As we moved into the cafeteria, Marsha was talking a mile a minute to Collette and Stacy. I hoped Stacy noticed that my insult had bounced right off her. From now on Marsha was safe from me. I didn't want Stacy to look at me that way again. Maybe she didn't understand my sense of humor? What if she didn't like my valentine? What if she thought it said she looked like an old wad of gum?

"Roger, you look like you're ready to throw up," said Patrick.

"Thanks," I said dryly. "You're looking pretty cool yourself."

Patrick started to laugh. "I bet you're just a little nervous about the dance on Friday, right?"

"Wrong," I lied. I didn't belong at a dance. What would I do in a school gym with loud music and a zillion paper hearts dangling from the ceiling? I'd probably get completely tangled in them, like a fly in a spiderweb.

Patrick and I grabbed trays and collected our lunch. Actually, I wasn't a bit hungry. There were so many knots in my stomach, there wasn't much room for food. Even chocolate pudding.

"I don't know about this valentine business," I said.

Patrick started laughing. "Whoa, calm down,

Roger. No one can make us go to that dance."

We sat down and I opened my milk, taking a long sip. Why did Stacy give me that look? I mean, it wasn't as if I had tried to set Marsha's scraggly hair on fire or anything.

Girls always stuck together. I better let them cool off for a few hours. Maybe a few weeks. Maybe a lifetime.

"We have to go to school one hundred and eighty days a year, Roger, and we have to return all library books," commented Patrick. "But we do not *have* to attend dances." Patrick took a big bite from his jelly sandwich and shrugged. "But, maybe we *should* go."

"What?"

Patrick nodded. "If we watch the sixth graders dance, we might learn how."

"I don't want to look like a jerk," I said.

"It will be dark, and no one will be looking at you anyway," Patrick pointed out. "Besides, nobody in the fifth grade knows how to dance. There aren't any rules like when our grandparents danced. Today it's just hopping around. My cousin showed me how. You don't even have to hold a girl's hand anymore. You don't have to touch one part of them."

"For slow dances you do," I said.

Patrick blushed. "Yeah, well, who says we have to slow dance?"

I shrugged. "What if some girl comes up to you and asks *you* to slow dance? Then what?"

Patrick let his sandwich drop with a dull *thwack*. He looked worried. "Hey, can they do that? Even if we're standing on our side of the gym?"

"Sure they can," I cried. "Girls can do whatever they want."

Patrick and I both leaned over and looked at the girls at the end of our table. Marsha was yakking away a mile a minute. Lots of girls were laughing. Even Stacy!

I sat up, feeling much better. Stacy looked happy now. Maybe her frown earlier wasn't because of my insult to Marsha. Maybe she had just been hungry. I smiled, feeling a little hungry myself. Stacy wasn't mad at me. The dance might not be such a bad idea after all.

"Listen to those girls laughing," said Patrick. "You're right, Roger. Those girls are definitely planning something. We better *not* go to the dance."

"We have to go!" I said. "It will be fun!"

"What?" Patrick dropped his sandwich again. "Make up your mind, Roger. One minute you hate anything connected with Valentine's Day, and the next minute you're begging me to go to some dance."

"I wasn't begging you." I tried to keep my voice calm, since a few kids were staring at us.

"Yes, you were!" shouted Patrick. "And I don't care what you say, I'm not going to the dance."

"Quiet down there," Marsha hollered.

I had my mouth open to shout back, "Mind your own business, Cessano!" when I noticed Stacy staring at me. So I just waved instead. Marsha looked disappointed, but Stacy waved back.

"You are acting so weird today," Patrick muttered. He tapped his fingers up and down on the table. "What's bugging you, anyway?"

All of a sudden, I felt a surge of confidence rush through me. Here I was, sitting next to my best friend, and the nicest girl in our school was smiling and waving at me. I felt great. Wonderful! I had to share my good news.

"Patrick," I began, proud that I hadn't even bothered to lower my voice. "I like a girl."

He looked confused. "You like *girls*?" asked Patrick.

I shook my head, ready to fill Patrick in on all the facts. "I like *a* girl, Patrick." I jerked my head toward the end of the table. "Voilà!"

Patrick peered past me, his eyes growing huge. "*Marsha?*" he yelped.

I shuddered. "No!"

Patrick leaned over, studying the girls at the end of the table. He was quiet for a long minute. "Stacy?"

"Yeah."

"She's nice."

"Real nice," I said. "I mean, I'm not going to ask her to the dance or anything."

"Better not. If you did, the whole school would know you like a girl. Even Sister Mary Elizabeth."

I put my head on the table. I didn't know what to do. Why did I think it would be so easy?

Valentine's Day can be murder!

6

Patrick and I were the first to race outside when the bell rang for recess. My stomach tightened the way it did when I got in the car to go to the dentist.

"Won't be long now, Roger," Patrick whispered. "In another few minutes, Stacy will walk over to her valentine box and the rest will be history. Move over, Romeo and Juliet."

"Patrick. Don't go making a big deal out of this. I just like her, that's all."

"Does she know?" Patrick asked. He crossed his arms. "I mean, did you ever actually confront her with your feelings?"

I shrugged, not knowing what to say. I wasn't a hundred percent sure of what *confront* even meant. But Patrick knew. I was so glad I told him. He's smart. I already felt like I was talking to a professional. Patrick must watch a lot of talk shows.

"Stacy doesn't know yet. Just you and me."

Patrick looked disappointed.

"But she'll know *soon*," I added quickly. "In minutes. I should have affronted her sooner."

"*Confronted*," corrected Patrick. "Go on."

"I mean, I just discovered I had a crush on her a few days ago. Then I wanted to make sure it wasn't some sort of twenty-four-hour thing."

Patrick nodded, rubbing his chin. "Good, good. So as of right now, the only people who know are the two of us. That's good. The fewer people who know, the better."

"Why?"

Patrick lowered his voice. "Now don't take this the wrong way, Rog, but Stacy may be way out of your league. And if that's the case, you don't want a lot of sixth graders making fun of you."

"For what?" The recess line started moving up the stairs to the school.

Patrick sighed. "Technically, for *liking a girl out of your league*."

"How do I know which league I'm in?" I wanted to know.

Patrick grabbed a small notebook from his back pocket and uncapped his pen. "Trust me, Roger. You're in the *beginners'* league." He grinned. "So am I. Most of the kids in the fifth grade are."

"What are you talking about?" Maybe I shouldn't have told him about liking Stacy.

"Relax, Roger," Patrick said. "Don't get nervous. You're lucky I have an older cousin in the eighth grade. She explained this *league* stuff at the Fourth of July picnic at Aunt Loretta's."

"Forget the league business, Patrick," I said quickly. "Stacy is very nice, okay? I just like her as a person. Just like I like your Aunt Loretta."

Patrick laughed. "Do you want to send my Aunt Loretta a mushy valentine?"

"Of course not!" Patrick's Aunt Loretta had to be forty!

"Do you want to dance with Aunt Loretta?" Patrick was scribbling away in his notebook. "All these facts add up, Roger."

I grabbed the notebook. "Patrick, I'm sorry I ever told you."

Patrick took his notebook back and jammed it into his pocket. "Excuse me for trying to help you sort out your messed-up life."

"It isn't messed up!" I insisted. "Nobody but you knows I even like Stacy!"

We both grew quiet as we walked around the playground. Why had I ever opened my mouth? Patrick elbowed me when Stacy raced by me, but I ignored him.

"I didn't mean to get you mad, Roger," said Patrick. "But trust me. My cousin knows what she's talking about. She's been to at least four dances."

"Oh, okay," I finally said. "What do I need to know?"

Patrick looked relieved that I was finally getting with the program. "Okay, so we know you are in the beginners' league. You have no track record with girls, no girls have ever liked you, and no girls are acting like they *might* like you."

I sat down on the top step. My life sounded pretty miserable. Maybe I belonged in a sub-beginners' league.

"So what are you saying, Patrick? I should send your Aunt Loretta a valentine?"

Patrick laughed. "Don't get discouraged. We just have to take things one step at a time. Now, the first step is to find out how Stacy feels about you." Patrick pointed to the hedges. "There she is."

I yanked his hand down. "Shhh. Don't even *think* about asking her, Patrick."

"I won't," agreed Patrick. "Besides, all we have to do is study her reaction to your valentine. It's as simple as that."

"You're right. Sounds simple to me."

Ten minutes later, when the bell rang to line up, I wasn't so sure.

7

Patrick and I stayed in the hall as long as possible, so Stacy would have enough time to go in and check her valentine box.

"Should we go in yet?" I whispered. I was on my fifth drink of water.

Patrick poked his head inside the classroom. When he turned back to me, he was smiling.

"Stacy likes it!" he said.

I hurried inside, whipping out my pencil and pretending to sharpen it while I searched the room. Stacy looked happy, all right. Maybe she'd keep this valentine forever.

"I can't believe it!" Stacy laughed.

"Let's read it again!" Marsha cried.

I frowned. Busybody, Marsha. Go shake your own valentine box and see how empty it is. The pencil sharpener whined as I sped up to ninety miles an hour. Maybe I should just go back there and hear what Stacy had to say.

I pulled my pencil stub from the sharpener and

tossed it in the trash can as I walked to the radiator. "Come on, Patrick. It's now or never."

"Well, what's going on?" I asked the girls. I spun the globe and looked everywhere but at Stacy.

"None of your business," Marsha sang out.

Stacy and Collette smiled at me and Patrick.

"Valentine's Day is off to a great start," said Stacy.

I tried to keep my smile under control but it kept getting bigger and bigger. I licked my front teeth and tried to unstick my upper lip.

Marsha waved the valentine under my nose, practically slashing off my left nostril. "Special delivery."

I glared at her, wishing I could special deliver her to the lost-and-found box in the furnace room.

"It's wonderful!" added Stacy.

I smiled at Stacy. "Great!" Glad you liked it, I wanted to add.

Marsha leaned against the radiator, fanning herself with Stacy's valentine. I shoved my hands in my pockets so I wouldn't snatch it away from her and return it to Stacy.

Marsha looked at me and frowned. "Don't you even try to read this, Roger."

"You shouldn't be reading it either," I snapped.

Marsha raised an eyebrow. "Why shouldn't I read it?"

"Because it's none of your business," I said.

"It's mine," cried Marsha, reaching out and whacking my arm with the valentine. "It's totally my business!"

"Yours?" I yelped. What was going on here? *That valentine was meant for Stacy.*

"It's lovely," said Stacy. "Marsha's first valentine. A boy sent her a funny poem."

"What?" I asked.

Marsha held the valentine up in the air as she marched back to her seat. I watched as she gave the valentine a huge kiss before putting it inside her desk.

Patrick patted me on the back as he went to his seat. Stacy and Collette went back and shook their valentine boxes one last time. They were empty.

I slunk back to my seat, feeling empty, too.

8

I sat in my seat a long time, wondering how in the world Marsha had ended up with Stacy's valentine. Maybe when I was at the globe, searching for a continent, I accidentally found Cessano. I shuddered. Now Marsha was holding Stacy's valentine prisoner in her desk. How was I going to get it out and back where it belonged?

The afternoon dragged on. During spelling, I finished a tattoo on my left thumb with a BIC pen. I drew circles, lots of them, all over my thumb. I added some eyes with a pair of glasses and suddenly had Mr. Potato Head smiling back at me.

"We're in deep trouble now, Mr. Potato Head," I whispered. "The fifth-grade grinch has stolen the valentine."

"Roger?"

Mrs. Pompalini was standing by my desk. She crossed her arms and frowned at me and Mr. Potato Head. "Go wash your hands and then come back and finish your assignment."

When I got back, the whole class was trying to write poems using our ten spelling words. Assignments like that were fun. They were much more fun than writing the same word fifty times.

"Do we have to use *all* ten words?" Marsha asked. "I think it might be impossible, Mrs. Pompalini."

"*You're* the one who is impossible, Marsha," I muttered as I slid into my seat.

Marsha glared at me. "Bet I can use more words than you."

Bet me that valentine, I wanted to shout.

Mrs. Pompalini tapped her yardstick against the chalkboard. "Roger, do you have any suggestions for Marsha?"

Sure, I thought. How about a long walk off a short pier?

I looked up at the board, chewing my lip. "Yeah, how about this. It reminds me of Marsha:

ROSES ARE A *CHARMING* RED,
FRAGRANT, *THORNY*, AND BLUE.
TOO BAD MY BATHROOM MIRROR BROKE,
WHEN IT *WITNESSED* UGLY YOU!"

Marsha kicked the back of my seat. Mrs. Pompalini frowned and told me to get back to work. I grinned over at Stacy, who was staring at me. I ducked my head. So, what did I do now? The poem wasn't that bad. I had used *four* spelling words.

"Just trying to help out," I muttered.

I had just used the seventh word when Marsha hissed at me. At first I ignored her, thinking she was just being Marsha. But she kept hissing, so I turned around.

Marsha was holding the valentine in front of her like a shield. "You better be careful around me, Roger," she hissed. "Or I'll ask my new boyfriend to beat you up!"

I spun around in my seat. Sure, Marsha. Like I'm going to punch myself in the nose!

Ten minutes later, I was finished with my poem. I had used all ten words, and it rhymed. I was getting pretty good at poetry writing. Most of the other kids in the class were still working on their poems. Even Collette, who always finished first, was busy writing.

I drummed my fingers up and down on my desk, wondering if I should write Stacy another poem. This time I would print her name on the outside, maybe add a skull and crossbones, and a Marsha-Keep-Out sign in the corner.

"Roger!" someone whispered.

It was Stacy! She smiled at me, then glanced up at Mrs. Pompalini before tossing a small white square of paper on my desk.

A note! Stacy had written me a note!

My hand flew on top of that note faster than a

bullfrog could hop on a fly. I lowered it to my lap and read:

> Dear Roger,
> Meet me at the lockers after school. We have to talk about the valentine card!
> Stacy

Stacy knew! She knew that card was meant for her and that I wrote it. I slid the note into my desk and glanced up at the clock. When the dismissal bell rang, I would tell her the whole story. Marsha from Mars might have my card, but Stacy would be my valentine.

9

When the dismissal bell rang, I shot out of my seat so fast a trail of smoke followed me out into the hall.

Stacy did not race out. In fact, she did not come out. I peered back inside the classroom, watching Stacy say good-bye to Marsha and Collette. I ducked back to my locker and pretended I was dusting off my tennis shoes.

Stacy was probably taking her time because she didn't want a crowd around. I finished dusting my tennis shoes and then got out a penny and tried to scrape off a wad of gum from my locker door. There was plenty to do in a locker if you really thought about it.

"Hey, Rog," said Stacy.

"So," I began. "The end of another school day." I opened and closed my locker a few times. I waited for Stacy to pick up the ball and carry it, but she didn't.

"Yes, here it is, dismissal time," I began again.

I swung my bookbag from my left to right shoulder. "The buses will be called any minute."

"That's right," Stacy agreed. She was putting her scarf into her bookbag.

"Yes, sir, the end of the day," I said cheerfully. I opened my locker again and straightened out my things. "The good old end of the day. After school."

Stacy looked down the hall. I closed my locker. Time was running out. Had she forgotten about the note?

"Roger," Stacy said at last. "I only have a minute."

"Hey," I said brightly. "Add sixty of them together and you have a whole hour."

Stacy blinked. "Excuse me?"

"So, what did you want to talk about?" I said. Give her the direct, non-funny approach.

"I've been thinking about Marsha's valentine card," said Stacy.

"Whoa," I said, laughing out loud. "I can explain it. It's pretty funny once you hear the whole story."

"Well, I think I *know* the whole story," Stacy said quietly. "I pieced it together, which is why I had to talk to you."

I drew in a deep breath and waited. Here it was.

"Roger, the way you and Marsha bicker back and forth has worried me a little."

I was trying to keep a smile on my face, but I couldn't understand what Marsha had to do with any of this. I wanted Stacy to get to the good stuff . . . the part where she tells me that she knows I like her and she likes me back. Who cared about Marsha?

"Back home I had an older cousin named Jeff who was forever teasing my baby-sitter, Dana. Sometimes he would tease her so bad she would just burst out crying. I figured they just didn't like each other, but then the next thing you knew he was being nice and told her he was in love with her. They got married last year."

My smile was struggling to hang on. Why was Stacy telling me about her baby-sitter getting married? Was I supposed to send her a toaster?

"So, great story. Listen, Stacy, I liked reading your note," I said. Maybe Stacy needed a nudge in the right direction. "You said you wanted to talk to me."

Stacy slung her bookbag over one shoulder. "It's probably none of my business . . ."

"It *is*!" I cried. My life *is* your business.

Stacy's eyes widened. "Well, thank you. I mean, I am a friend of yours and . . ."

"You're a *great* friend," I agreed.

Stacy smiled. "And I am Marsha's friend, too."

I grinned. "At least she has *one*, then."

Stacy shook her head. "See, there you go again. This is the very reason I wanted to talk to you.

You've got to stop teasing Marsha. It's going to just ruin the most special Valentine's Day of all."

"I'm sorry," I said. "If it makes you happy, I'll stop teasing her. I'll even send her a valentine."

Stacy looked pleased. "Another one?"

"What?" How did Stacy know that was my card?

"Roger, you can stop pretending with me. I know you sent Marsha that valentine. When you read that poem in class, I recognized your style. You like Marsha, admit it. She's your *special* girl."

"What?" I shrieked. "Marsha isn't a bit special. And the lab results might be in any second proving she isn't even a girl."

As the second group of buses were called, I reached out and tried to grab onto Stacy's arm. She was laughing and waving her finger at me.

"Now, you just stop all that teasing and be nice to Marsha," Stacy ordered. "And from now on, sign your valentine cards."

"Stacy, I didn't send that card to Marsha. I can't stand her. Trust me! Ask her. Ask anyone in the whole school. Even the cafeteria ladies know how I feel. I tried to slip a dead fly into her banana pudding in the third grade!"

"I'll be watching you now, Rog!" Stacy called as she hurried toward the door. "Back in Santa Fe, a gentleman does not insult his lady."

"You don't understand," I whispered. As I watched Stacy disappear into the crowd, my mouth fell open and my heart cracked.

I moved like a robot down the hall toward my bus. As I passed the bulletin board by Sister Mary Elizabeth's office, I stopped. The dance! Valentine's Day. The whole mess had begun right here. Why didn't Cupid mind his own business? Why didn't he just shoot himself in the foot if he felt like shooting arrows?

Suddenly, I went nuts. I dropped my bookbag and tore the red heart announcing the dance from the bulletin board. I crumpled it up and threw it on the floor. With my left foot I whacked it down the hall like a soccer ball. It felt great. I turned back and pried Cupid from the board. I put my hands around his thin paper neck and strangled him. Mind your own business, Cupid!

I was in the middle of biting off Cupid's left leg when Sister Mary Elizabeth stormed out of her office.

10

"**R**oger Friday, *what* are you doing?" cried Sister Mary Elizabeth.

I dropped Cupid's wrinkled red body. "I'm sorry, Sister Mary Elizabeth," I said quickly. I stood up straighter and looked her right in the eye. "I just couldn't seem to help myself."

"You seldom can," Sister muttered. She lowered her glasses and rubbed her eyes. "I was hoping second semester of the fifth grade would be a fresh start for you, Roger."

"It is," I agreed. "Have I smuggled in one dead snake since last semester?"

"No," Sister had to admit.

"Which proves I don't want to get in any more trouble," I continued. "I have walked past this bulletin board twenty times without touching it."

"You were never supposed to touch it," pointed out Sister. "A bulletin board is not a hands-on activity."

"But it's all wrong, Sister."

43

"Well, it certainly is wrong now, Roger." Sister pushed her glasses up a notch and looked at the board. "What have you done?"

I glanced down at the crinkled red paper by my feet. "Cupid was all wrong for the job, Sister." I drew in a deep breath and smiled.

Sister did not smile back. Sister closed her eyes for a long minute. "I pray that you do have a point, Mr. Friday. You are about to miss your bus and I am about to lose my patience."

I nodded. "I'll talk fast, Sister. When I walked past this bulletin board, I saw red. And it wasn't just because of all the hearts."

Sister looked puzzled. "What exactly upset you?"

"Valentine's Day is a reminder to be nice to everyone, right?"

"Correct."

"So Cupid just stood here, not saying a word."

"He's made of paper, Roger. What do you expect him to say?"

I shifted my bookbag to my other shoulder. "Why not have a *real* poem on this bulletin board? Not just a cartoon character."

My bus was being called for the second time.

"Roger, what exactly are you trying to say?"

I had absolutely no idea.

"Roger, why did you willfully destroy this bulletin board?" asked Sister, shoving her glasses up another notch.

"I . . . I just wanted it to be right," I said. "I wanted Cupid to bite the dust to make room for the real meaning of love."

"Which is what?"

"A poem. A real old-fashioned poem, like the one about stopping by a snowy farm and wondering who lived there."

Sister nodded. "Robert Frost — a wonderful poet."

"Exactly, Sister! Exactly my point!" I was talking so fast I was spitting. "And if Robert, I mean Mr. Frost, saw Cupid here representing love, instead of a good poem, why he'd . . . he'd never write again."

"He'll never write again, Roger. He's dead."

That stopped me for a second, but not for two. "Yeah, which is even more of a reason to replace stupid Cupid with a real good poem."

"What exactly did you have in mind, Roger?"

"Well," I began. I had nothing in mind.

"Surely you had some poem ready to put up here when you furiously removed the existing Cupid."

"I did!" I said. "I'm just about ready for the final draft. Mrs. Pompalini always says, 'There are no good writers, only good rewriters'!" I laughed.

Sister did not laugh. She crossed her arms and looked down at the rumpled bit of red that was once Cupid.

I had to act fast. Any minute now Sister would scoop up Cupid's destroyed body and suspend me from Sacred Heart forever.

"Sister, I was thinking more of a poem that would remind every student at Sacred Heart Elementary that love is the way to go. The bus to take, the . . ."

Sister closed her eyes again. This time she didn't open them. "Speaking of buses, yours is about to leave. Get on your bus, Mr. Friday, and make sure you have a poem for me tomorrow morning." Sister opened her eyes. "I want it hanging on the bulletin board by eight o'clock, Roger, and I want it to be *good*. In fact, I want it to be *outstanding*. Your poem cannot start with 'Roses are red,' or you will be sitting in my office at eight-o-five, do you understand?"

I smiled, nodded, and then ran to my bus.

So okay, I talked faster than my mind could think. So I promised a poem that would replace Cupid in history.

I could do it. Maybe. I groaned as I ran to my bus. I had to do it. What choice did I have? Unless I found a way to turn myself into Robert Frost by morning, I was going to have a very short shelf life at Sacred Heart Elementary. And if I got kicked out, then I'd never get to hang out with my best friend, Patrick, or find out if someone as nice as Stacy thought I was nice, too. The bottom line was, if Sister Mary Elizabeth called my par-

46

ents once more this year to announce that I had messed up, I would never, ever get finished serving detention. I would be too busy scraping gum off the gym bleachers to attend my own high school graduation.

11

"**R**oger, tell your Gram what's wrong."

I glanced up from my thick slice of chocolate cake and tried to muster a smile for my grandmother. "I guess I'm just tired."

Gram reached out and patted my hand. "I was so excited when your parents called and asked me to come watch you and Becky for a few days. Why, I had my mixer out and plugged in before I even hung up the phone."

"When will they be back?" I asked. I stabbed at my cake, wondering if Sister could throw me out of school and church all in one great swoop. I'd have to wait in the car while my parents went to Mass each Sunday.

"They'll be back Saturday morning," Gram said. "Too bad your mother's aunt died so suddenly, but lucky for me I get to be with my two favorite grandchildren."

I smiled, even though my life was about to take a nose dive. Gram only *had* two grandchildren.

"Gram, did my dad ever get into trouble in school?" I asked. Maybe if I had a good story on my dad, I could bring it up while he was yelling at me. I could remind him I was just a chip off the old block.

Gram laughed. "Heavens, no!"

I dropped my fork and slumped back in my chair. So much for the chip theory. Maybe I had been chopped off a troublesome block.

"Was I switched at birth?" I asked.

Gram took a few bites and poured herself some milk. "Your dad never got in much trouble. I think his biggest problem was in the fifth grade."

I sat back up. "That's great! What happened in the fifth grade?" This was terrific. I could tell my dad how hard fifth grade was. It was a year that even perfect, unfunny people got in trouble. It was probably all tied up with hormones!

"That was the year, all right," Gram went on. "Your dad lost a library book and had to pay for it. He was so upset, I thought he was going to have a stroke. He got a job sweeping out the laundromat and paid the whole fine by himself. He walked two miles to the laundromat and back for over a week to earn the money."

My head slumped down on the kitchen table. Oh, great. My father probably walked through waist-high snow and then swept the laundromat by candlelight. I was going to have to explain the murder of Cupid to Abe Lincoln.

"You okay, Rog?" Gram asked again.

"Yes," I muttered. But I wasn't. My parents were going to be so disappointed . . . again. They had been so upset about me bringing in a dead snake earlier in the year that I had promised them both that I was going to try harder. And I had tried.

I sighed. Trying should count for more than it did.

I sighed again. I should have let poor Cupid alone.

"I got in a little bit of trouble at school today, Gram."

Gram stood up. She was suddenly all grand-mother. "So exactly what kind of trouble are we talking about?"

"I ripped up Cupid, and then Sister told me to write a Robert Frost-like poem about love or else I was going to get a one-way ticket out of Sacred Heart."

Gram's eyebrows went up.

"Sister is nice, Gram, but I think she's tired of me getting in so much trouble. She's a nun. She promised to love God and all His people, but I think my warranty is about to expire. Sister says I have to have that poem hanging from the bulletin board by eight o'clock tomorrow morning or else."

Gram gave me a quick hug and then stood up tall. "Or else, huh? Well, there is nothing to worry about, Roger. By the time your parents get home, this whole thing will be Wednesday's wash. They don't have to know."

I nodded. I didn't care when we did our laundry, but it sounded like Gram was saying we wouldn't have to tell my parents. I liked that part.

"You're a funny boy, Roger, and you love to read. So that combination tells me that you have the makings of being a good writer."

"I can't write a poem good enough for Sister Mary Elizabeth," I said.

"Says who?"

I shrugged. "I don't know."

"Of course you don't know," Gram insisted. "You won't know till you try to write that poem. Now you run along and start writing. I'll clean up the dishes and go get your sister Becky."

"Thanks, Gram."

She grinned at me. "For the cake?"

"For everything." I walked slowly back to my room, willing to try to write the poem, but knowing that I might be writing myself out of Sacred Heart.

12

I sat down at my desk and started writing. In less than an hour, I had ten rotten poems. I picked my best, which was still pretty bad.

VALENTINE'S DAY IS A NICE DAY.
PEOPLE TRY HARD TO GET OUT OF
YOUR WAY.
IF YOU ARE IN LOVE, YOU GET CANDY.
PEOPLE LIKE THE CARAMELS BEST,
SAYING THEY ARE DANDY.

Gram knocked on the door and poked her head in the room. "How's it going, Roger?

I showed her my poem.

"Why, I think you might be on to something, dear," said Gram. "Valentine's Day is about getting candy, but it's about getting out of people's way. Being polite and thoughtful."

"Is that what I said?" It was beginning to sound like a poem Sister would like.

Gram put the paper back down on my desk. "So now that you know what you want to say, write it again and it will be easier."

I got out a new sheet of paper.

VALENTINE'S DAY IS FILLED
WITH CANDY
BUT, ALSO FILLED WITH PEOPLE
BEING KIND.
JUST LIKE IN A BOX OF CHOCOLATES,
YOU NEVER KNOW WHAT
YOU WILL FIND.

I felt so good after writing that poem, I decided to try one last time writing Stacy a poem. It wasn't going to be a bulletin-board poem, but one that would make her smile. After four or five tries, I came up with this:

EVER SINCE YOU SMILED AT ME
I'VE BEEN HAPPY AND VERY CAREFREE.
CHOCOLATE IS SWEET AND GOOEY, TOO.
BUT, VALENTINE, NOBODY CAN
OUT FUDGE YOU!

I got out my markers and made a border around Stacy's poem. It wasn't fancy, just a heart in each corner, and a little bit of grass growing along the sides. My hearts looked a little bit like rocks, but my grass looked exactly like grass blowing in the wind. I folded Stacy's poem into a neat square and put it in my bookbag. Next, I went into my sister Becky's room and paid her fifty cents to make a huge red heart for the bulletin-board poem. She charged me an extra ten cents to add red glitter. I figured it was worth sixty cents to pass fifth grade.

The next morning my bus pulled up in front of the school at exactly ten minutes to eight. As I raced up the stairs to meet my deadline, my stomach felt alive, as if I had swallowed a jar full of moths.

"Wait up, Roger," called Patrick. "You're trying to run the three-minute mile. What's up with you?"

"I have to have this valentine poem on Sister's bulletin board by eight o'clock or I'm in trouble."

Patrick grinned. "You wrote Sister a poem? You didn't ask her to be your valentine, did you?"

"No," I said. "Cupid took an unexpected leave of absence so I offered to help fill the space."

"Offered?"

I grinned. "Plea-bargained is more like it. I lost my temper and Cupid lost his leg."

I reached in my folder and pulled out both poems. "Here. Hold these while I tack up the heart for Sister's bulletin board."

"Looks good, Roger."

"Thanks. Wait here a second, Patrick. I'm going to run to the office and borrow the stapler."

The school's secretary, Miss Merkle, was happy to see me. I've been sent to the school office about a trillion times since kindergarten, so we're pretty good friends now.

"Have a peppermint, Roger. How's your mother?"

"Fine, Miss Merkle. How's your dog? Did she ever have those puppies?"

"Yes. Ten little golden retrievers." Miss Merkle pulled out her center drawer and got out a packet of pictures. "Let me show you a few snapshots."

I glanced at them quickly, then borrowed the stapler. I didn't want to be a second late for Sister. "See you later, Miss Merkle."

"I hope I don't see you too soon." She laughed.

I hurried down the hall. Only two more minutes before Sister would appear. I chuckled to myself. Gram convinced me that Sister Mary Elizabeth would be very impressed with my poem. "Oh, Roger," she would say. "I mean, *Mr.* Roger Frost Friday. You are a fine poet. In fact, you are the most wonderful boy in the whole school."

When I arrived at the bulletin board, there was a small crowd. A sixth grader named Nate Nelson and a few of his friends were talking to Patrick.

"So let me read the other one," said Nate. "Come on. What's it going to hurt? I already read one."

"Hey," I said. "What's up?"

Patrick looked a little nervous. Nate was practically six feet tall and growing every second.

"I want to read the other poem," said Nate. "Your friend here said you wrote them, Friday. Tell him to hand it over." Nate was probably the coolest kid in the sixth grade, so he wasn't about to waste any manners on me.

I smiled and took the glittered paper from Patrick's clammy hands, stapling it to the center of the bulletin board. "There, now everyone can read it."

"I already read this one," said Nate. "Pete said the other one is funny."

"It's *Patrick*," corrected Patrick.

"You read the other poem?" I asked. "Patrick, I asked you to *hold* them, not memorize them."

Nate laughed. "Funny, that's very funny. So tell your friend to hand over the poem."

"It's private," I said quickly. I took the poem from Patrick and shoved it into my pocket. Nate's hand closed around my arm. He was so tall he could have reeled me in like a trout.

"So what's a little fifth grader like yourself doing with a private poem?" asked Nate. "You have a girlfriend or something?"

"It's nothing serious," reported Patrick. "The girl doesn't even know and . . ."

"Patrick!" I snapped.

Nate laughed. "That's cool. Listen, since this girl doesn't even know she's your girlfriend, maybe you'd let me buy that poem."

"Buy it?"

Nate dropped my arm. "Yeah, I need a quick poem to give my own girlfriend. The cards in the stores are too mushy. I want something funny. You're a funny guy. Want to make a few bucks?"

I glanced at the clock near the office. Any minute now Sister would come marching down the hall to see my poem. She would love to see a crowd reading it, but would not be a bit pleased to find me selling poems in the school hall. Even the Girl Scouts weren't allowed to sell cookies during school hours. Time was running out, and I didn't know what to do!

13

"I'll give you three bucks," Nate offered.

My mouth fell open. "Three bucks? You want to give me *three bucks* for a poem?"

"Yeah. I've been looking for a good valentine for over a week. I don't want too much gushy mush. I don't want to marry the girl."

"Sixth grade is a little young, Nate," I admitted. "You'd have to ask your *parents* to drive you to the church."

Patrick laughed. Nate glared at him, so Patrick turned around and pretended to be reading my poem.

"You're kind of a wise guy," muttered Nate. He bent down to stare at me some more. "Are you sure you wrote that poem?"

I blushed, then coughed. "Hey," I stammered. "I am Roger Friday, right? You see the name on the poem, right?"

Nate nodded. "Yeah. So what do you say? I'll

make it three dollars and fifty cents and that's it. Final offer."

"Well . . ." I patted my pocket. "This is a pretty good poem, all right. Poems that don't rhyme usually start at four dollars. I don't think Robert Frost ever sold one of his poems for less than ten dollars."

Nate moved closer and closed his hand over mine and the stapler. His hand was the size of a dinner plate. "You better sell me that poem, or Robert Frost might just start nippin' at your nose a little early this year. Now are you going to sell me the poem, or should I just staple *you* to the bulletin board?"

"Ha, ha," I said. Nate was known as a pretty laid-back kind of guy, but I had already learned that the right girl would make a guy do strange things. I glanced down at his huge hand. Any minute now Stacy would be walking by and find me stapled in the center of the perfect heart my sister made.

"Hey," I said. "Just joking, Nate. Poets joke a lot." With my free hand I reached in my pocket and handed Nate the poem. "Here, three fifty it is."

Nate took the poem and handed me three dollars. "Oh, look at this. I only have three bucks. Lucky for me this poem just went on sale."

Nate and his friends walked away with my

poem. I glanced down at the three dollars, not really knowing what to think. Should I be happy I sold my first poem, or just relieved that I wasn't hanging from the bulletin board?

"Whoa, that Nate is big," Patrick said. "Who made him boss of the whole school?"

"I think his forty-inch neck has something to do with it," I explained. "I didn't want to sell him that poem. I had plans for it."

"I'm sorry, Roger. It was kind of my fault. I guess I should have kept them both in your folder," said Patrick. "At least you can write another one. I had no idea you were so good at poetry."

"Why, Mr. Friday," said Sister. She started smiling as she walked toward us. "The bulletin board looks wonderful. I see the poem is in place. I can hardly wait to read it."

The more Sister read, the bigger her smile got. By the time she finished it, she bent down and actually hugged me. Sister had never hugged me before, except at Christmastime when I gave her some bath salts from my mother.

"Oh, this is wonderful, Roger. You were right. Cupid is fine, but this poem . . ." Sister took a step back and smiled at the poem. She stretched out her arms, and for a second I thought she was going to hug the poem as well. But she just clapped her hands together. "This poem has captured the true sense of giving. I am very proud of you, Roger!"

Before I could get another word out, Sister took off down the hall to yell at two third graders who were playing with the water fountain.

Seconds later, the morning bell rang. The next thing I knew, Patrick and I were swept down the hall by a hundred kids. I turned and gave my poem one final glance. It was just there, in the heart, looking fine. How was I to know how much trouble it was going to cause?

14

By lunchtime, I was as famous as you could get at Sacred Heart without being related to the Pope. People kept coming up to compliment me on the great poem. Even the gym teacher, who never talks to anyone. A cafeteria worker gave me an extra oatmeal raisin cookie, and a cool eighth-grade girl with curly blond hair came up to me and said I had talent.

"You're a celebrity," said Patrick as we sat down in the cafeteria.

"Thanks." I unwrapped my sandwich. Gram would be so happy to hear how many people loved my poetry.

"Roger, can I talk to you?"

"Hey, Stacy," said Patrick.

"Stacy!" I dropped my sandwich. Stacy was standing next to my table, holding her lunch tray. I tried to swallow fast, wondering if I should ask her to join us for lunch.

"Didn't mean to interrupt your lunch, but I just

wanted to tell you how much I liked your poem."

"Thanks."

"Rog, are you going to the dance on Friday?" asked Stacy. "I kind of . . . well, I wondered."

Patrick choked on his milk.

"Maybe," I said. "I mean, I'm not sure yet. I . . . I may stay home and write some more poetry."

Stacy laughed. "Maybe you should go to the dance and then write a poem about *that*."

"Yeah, maybe." I set my milk down. I liked Stacy so much, I felt nervous around her.

"I know a *certain girl* who would like to see you there," added Stacy.

Patrick's mouth fell open. Mine didn't. I knew Stacy was talking about Marsha.

"Well, I better go eat," said Stacy. "I hope to see you both at the dance."

"Sure," said Patrick. "I might lift a few weights and then head over."

As soon as Stacy left, I elbowed Patrick. "Since when did you start lifting?"

"About the same time you sat home to write poetry."

We both laughed.

"So, are you going to the dance?" asked Patrick.

I shrugged. "Maybe, maybe not."

"Stacy came right out and *asked* you to meet her there!"

"Not really. She said 'a certain girl.' I think she means Marsha."

Patrick laughed. "Trust me, she doesn't. Marsha can't stand you."

"I know, but . . ." I sighed, wishing I didn't have to tell Patrick about the valentine card mix-up. The fewer people who knew, the better. "I *accidentally* put the valentine card I made for Stacy in Marsha's box. Now Marsha thinks she has a boyfriend."

Patrick didn't laugh. "So, did you tell her?"

"I tried to tell Marsha it was a mistake, but she didn't believe me. Now Stacy thinks I *like* Marsha."

Patrick straightened his tie. "We are talking serious here, Roger. You've got to formulate a plan. First, send, no, fax, Marsha *another* card, telling her that you no longer like her. Tell . . . tell her it was . . . a twenty-four-hour kind of thing. Like the flu."

It sounded like a good plan. I wouldn't even have to sign my name. Just tell her that it was nice while it lasted, but it's over and she should go on with her life, without me.

"Hey, Rog!"

Nate Nelson stood in front of me.

"Listen, I recopied your poem," said Nate. "And I was wondering if you could do me *two* favors?"

I nodded, wondering if anyone would say no to someone the size of a redwood tree.

Nate handed me a piece of paper and a pencil. "First favor, I want you to add a verse to the poem I already bought from you. Write something to say that this girl has to meet me at the dance. Yeah, and that's when she finds out *I'm* the one sending her this valentine."

"Okay," I said, jotting down a few notes. "Sounds like a good plan, Nate. Where do you want to meet her? By the front door, by the punch bowl?"

"No. Definitely not the punch bowl, too crowded." Nate turned to Patrick. "Where do you think?"

"The Empire State Building," Patrick suggested.

"How about under the clock by the gym?" I suggested. "At eight o'clock?"

Nate smiled. "Yeah, under the clock at eight. Don't be late!"

I forced out a laugh as I began to scribble. "Good line, Nate. See, you don't really need me at all anymore."

"Yeah, I do," said Nate. "One last favor."

I held up the poem for Nate's approval. "Sure. One last favor."

Nate studied the poem.

MEET ME UNDER
THE CLOCK AT EIGHT.

SAVE ME TWO DANCES
AND PLEASE DON'T BE LATE!

Nate grinned. "This is perfect. Now for the last favor. Don't say no to this, Roger."

Patrick grabbed his milk carton and drained it. "What is it?"

Nate handed me back his poem. "Put this in her valentine box. She's in your homeroom, and I'm afraid someone might see me if I do it."

I nodded, sure that anyone almost six feet tall would be noticed. "Sure, who is she?"

Nate leaned down and put one huge hand on my shoulder. "Stacy Trinidad."

Maybe it was the weight of Nate's hand, or the shock of realizing I was arranging a love match between the coolest kid in the school and the girl of my dreams. But I took a nosedive into my banana cream pudding, and I wasn't sure if I wanted to come up for air.

15

"Gross move," muttered Nate as he walked away. "Don't forget to deliver that valentine."

By the time I had removed the pudding from my face, I had ten minutes to sneak down the hall and back into homeroom. Sister Mary Elizabeth patrols the halls with her zoom lens eyeballs, looking for any kid dumb enough to try and go back to his locker for a football or jacket.

"I'll wait for you outside, Roger," said Patrick. "Sister will spot a crowd for sure."

"I'll be right out," I promised. The thought of getting into trouble made Patrick nervous. Besides, I had gotten myself into this mess alone. I folded Nate's note in half, and then half again, trying to make it bite size. If I was spied by Sister, I could always swallow it before being captured.

Getting past the monitors on the lower level was easy. The boys' bathroom is past the stairs, and people never question you if you shout, "Rest room," and hop from foot to foot.

Today, I shot up the stairs and stuck my head around the corner. The hall was empty. I glanced to the left and saw that the door leading to Sister's inner office was closed. Miss Merkle was typing, but even if she saw me, she'd pretend she didn't.

I sped around the corner and hurried down the hall. I slowed as I passed the third-grade classroom, since the door was open. Luckily, Mrs. Byrnes was in the middle of lining the kids up for a spelling bee, so I slid past. Within another minute I was alone inside my own homeroom.

I walked over to Stacy's valentine box and shook it. Still empty. I pulled out Nate's valentine, wondering if he would ever find out if I just dropped it in the trash can instead. Why couldn't he like a girl from his own grade and leave Stacy alone?

I plunked the valentine in and turned to go.

"What are *you* doing here?"

I jumped, reaching out for the first thing I could think of, which was the globe. "I . . ."

Marsha stomped over, hands on hips.

"You're not *allowed* to be in here," she snapped.

"Neither are you," I snapped back. "You're too short and too dumb to be a teacher."

Marsha held up a key. "Oh, I have *permission*, something you don't have and can't even spell."

I grinned. Marsha was funny in her messed-up way.

"Mrs. Pompalini locked my allergy medication in the desk drawer, and I have to take it," announced Marsha. "I don't want to be sick for the dance."

I set the globe down. "Yeah, well, Mrs. Pompalini asked me to make sure Africa was still on the globe, and it is." I patted the globe.

"You're lying," said Marsha.

"No, really, here it is," I pointed to Africa. "In fact, it's shaped a little bit like that wart on your nose."

Marsha's hand flew up to her nose. As she lowered it, her eyes were all shiny, like she was about to cry.

"I was *kidding*," I said. "You don't have a wart. Do you?"

Marsha shook her head. "It's a mole. Does it really look like Africa?"

I took a step closer. There was a tiny black dot on the side of Marsha's nose. I had never noticed it. Maybe when she sneered at me, it didn't show.

"Nah, looks like a little ant, that's all."

Marsha groaned and slumped on a desktop. "Maybe I should have it taken off before the dance. What if my new boyfriend thinks I have ants crawling on my face?"

I laughed. "Pretend you just came from a picnic."

"It isn't funny," Marsha snapped. "This is very upsetting, Roger. I don't even know who this guy is. Maybe he's watching me while I'm eating my lunch."

"That's a scary thought," I said. "Maybe you should try chewing with your mouth closed from now on."

Marsha stood up and put her hands on her hips. "What am I doing talking to you? You don't know the first thing about having a valentine."

I sighed. Marsha was right about that!

"Oops, sorry." Marsha's cheeks were pink, and she really did look sorry. "I guess I was just being excited about my own card, and . . ."

"That's all right," I said as I headed for the door. "There's always next year."

"Yeah," Marsha agreed. "Too bad Valentine's Day can't be three times a year. Maybe four."

I closed the door and walked down the hall. If Valentine's Day came any more frequently, I'd be locked in a padded cell.

16

When I walked in from recess, Marsha was wearing a Band-Aid across her nose.

"What happened to you?" I asked.

"Shhhh." She grabbed my arm. "I don't want my boyfriend to call me 'bug face.' I'll wear some of my mom's makeup at the dance."

I shook my head, feeling a little guilty all of a sudden. What if Marsha took a good look in the mirror and discovered she had ten or twenty freckles, too? Would she come to the dance wrapped as a mummy?

I was going to have to pretend I was Marsha's boyfriend long enough to write her a note saying good-bye. But it was going to be harder now that she was covering up her warts and moles. Marsha was loony enough to think she was being dumped because she was turning into a bug. Even though Marsha was a pain in the neck, I didn't want her to end up in the funny farm thinking she was turning into some sort of beetle.

I got out my books for math and yawned. Valentine's Day was wearing me out. Today was Thursday, which meant the Valentine Dance was only a day away. Within twenty-four hours I had to write Marsha an exit poem, and then find a way to live with the fact that Nate and Stacy would become Sacred Heart's most famous couple.

By the time the dismissal bell rang, Marsha had added a second bandage to her nose, and I had a huge headache.

"Roger?"

Stacy stood in front of my desk. "Can I talk to you for a minute?"

"Sure," I said.

"Listen," Stacy began, dropping her voice to a whisper. "I . . . I found the valentine you wrote in *my* box."

"What?" I squeaked. "Me? I wrote you something?" My mind raced around and around like a gerbil wheel. Had I signed Roger at the end of the clock poem? Nate would kill me!

Stacy laughed. "Well, you didn't sign it, but I recognized your style."

"I . . . I don't know what you're talking about," I stammered. "I don't even have style."

Stacy grinned, her dimples working overtime. "You didn't sign the card, but I knew it was from you, so I helped you out a little."

"You did?"

"Yes," Stacy said. "You accidentally put it in

my box, but I knew you meant it for Marsha." Stacy put her hand on my arm. "You took my advice, Roger. That means a lot to me."

"It does?" I stared at her perfect hand. Her fingernails were painted a pale pink.

"So I put the card in Marsha's valentine box, and . . ."

"You what?" I shouted, rising from my seat.

"Yipeeeee!" shrieked Marsha from the radiator. She was clutching Nate's card to her heart as she spun around in a circle. "I have a date! My first date!"

Stacy grinned. "You have made her very happy, Roger."

"Wait!" I cried, but I already knew it was too late. The pin of the grenade had been pulled and it was sailing through space as I stood there. Come tomorrow night at eight, it would explode!

17

On the bus ride home from school I slumped down so low in my seat, I almost disappeared. My chin was resting on my knees as I watched Marsha in the front of the bus jabbering away to Collette about her mystery-man valentine.

"Listen to this, Collette. My boyfriend *insists* that I meet him under the clock at eight," Marsha repeated for the tenth time. "Now, do you think I should be *early*, which would show him that I'm excited, or should I be fashionably *late*, so he won't think I'm overly anxious?"

"How about meeting him at *eight* o'clock," suggested Collette. "So he knows you can follow instructions?"

"Oh, Collette!" Marsha laughed. "I don't think normal rules are used when you're dating. Daters have their own *special* rules. I wonder if the library has a book about dating?" Marsha leaned her head against the window. "I can't believe I am actually going to meet him tomorrow. This is like a dream come true. I just wish my moles would disappear."

My worst nightmare, I sighed. I closed my eyes, wondering if it would be Nate, or perhaps an enraged Marsha, who would actually kill me. Perhaps they would work as a team, or maybe Nate would snap me in two and they would each have a half to strangle.

"What are you going to say to him, Marsha?" asked Collette.

Marsha swung her head around. "Say?"

"Yes, when he comes up to you at the clock. I think it's very important to start things off on the right foot."

Marsha leaned closer. "I never thought about that. I guess I just thought he would say, 'Hi, do you want to dance?' and I would say, 'Yes, and . . .'"

I leaned forward, too. And . . .

Marsha covered her face. "And then I don't know what to say. Oh, Collette, what if he thinks I'm boring?"

I shuddered. Insane, yes. Boring! No chance. Nate won't think you're boring, Marsha, he will think you are the wrong person. Once Nate found Marsha, instead of Stacy, waiting under the clock, he would be furious. It would be a shock to his system, like ordering steak and getting chopped spinach.

"Roger, relax!" said Patrick. "So Marsha got the wrong valentine. No big deal."

"I consider *life* a big deal, Patrick. And unless I can find a way to get Stacy under that clock, and Marsha away from it, mine may be shortened."

Patrick was quiet for a few minutes. Finally he smiled. "All you have to do is send Marsha another valentine, canceling the clock date, then stick a valentine in Stacy's desk, pretending you're Nate, asking Stacy to meet you under the clock at eight."

It sounded so simple, I clung to it. It would work, of course it would. People cancel plans all the time.

Patrick handed me a sheet of paper and uncapped his pen. "Okay Roger. Go ahead!"

I thought for a second. "Okay — how about . . .

CANCEL THE DATE,
I'VE CHANGED MY MIND.
I'VE GOT THE FLU,
AND A BROKEN SPINE."

Patrick smiled. "It will work."

I frowned. "No. Marsha will be looking for someone in traction."

"Do you think there's any chance you could just explain to Nate that this weird girl has a crush on him and would he please dance with her?"

A flare of hope shot out of me, lighting up the dark cloud which had been following me. "Yeah, maybe he would do it. It's only one dance."

Patrick smiled, then frowned and shook his head. "No, on second thought, Nate would not do that, Roger."

"Why not?" I cried. "I love that plan, Patrick."

"Yeah, but it's doomed from the start. Remember all that league stuff I told you about? Well, sorry buddy, but it works both ways. Marsha is not even *close* to Nate's league. His last girlfriend was Jen Slane, a *seventh grader*. Zillions of girls have a crush on Nate."

We both sighed, picturing Jen. She was the prettiest girl in the seventh grade, maybe the whole school. Not only did she have long, shiny dark hair and beautiful eyes, but she was happy all the time. Nate wouldn't put up with Marsha after going with Jen.

"Maybe I could bribe Nate into dancing with Marsha," I whispered. "I heard him say he was saving up for a baseball card show."

Patrick looked encouraged. "Okay, okay. How much money do you have?" he asked.

"Four bucks," I said.

"It's going to take a lot more than that," muttered Patrick.

I agreed. And I didn't have any more money or any more time. Tonight I would have to write two more poems. One for Stacy asking her to meet

Nate at eight, and one final exit verse for Marsha.

The bus pulled up to the curb and stopped. Marsha flew off, her feet barely touching the aisle. I got up slowly, dragging my bookbag. You can do it, Roger old buddy, I muttered to myself. There's always one final card up your sleeve. I prayed hard that the card left was an ace.

18

That night I reached for the phone three times.
First, I was going to call a mental health hot-
line number I found in the phone book. I wanted
to explain my problem and see if they had any
solutions. I hung up after the first ring. What if
Sister Mary Elizabeth was a volunteer and recognized my voice?

"Roger Friday! Is that you?" she would shout.
"Get off this phone and let someone with a *real*
problem use it!"

The second time I was going to call Marsha,
pretending to be her mystery-man valentine.
"Hey, sorry to call on such short notice, Marsha,
but my parents won the lottery and we are moving
to Beverly Hills immediately." But the way my
luck was running, I knew my sister, Becky, would
pick up the phone asking, "Roger, who are you
talking to now?"

The last time was to call Patrick. I needed his
help. I was so tired the only two words I could

rhyme were *valentine* and *crime*. Being in charge
of four hearts — Marsha's, Nate's, Stacy's, and
mine — was exhausting! One wrong move would
crack any one of them, not to mention my neck if
Nate decided to stuff me in a locker.

"Wish I could come over, but it's my dad's birth-
day," said Patrick. "But stick with it. You can do
it."

At nine o'clock, I wrote the poems. The Valentine Dance would be starting in less than
twenty-four hours. I stuck the poems inside my
backpack, brushed my teeth, and prayed that a
blizzard would whip through Pittsburgh dropping
three feet of snow.

With the lights off, my two newest poems
echoed in the dark room.

DEAR MARSHA, MY VALENTINE,
I HOPE YOU ARE WELL
AND FEELING FINE.
DON'T LOOK FOR ME
AT THE DANCE TONIGHT,
DON'T TAKE IT PERSONALLY
AND MAKE THIS A FIGHT.
I HURT MY FOOT, IT'S BLACK AND BLUE,
WHICH MEANS I CAN'T COME
AND BE WITH YOU.

I bit my lip in the dark, hoping the poem
sounded convincing enough. I didn't want to hurt

Marsha's feelings; I just wanted to get her out from under the clock.

I sat up in bed and looked out at the moonlight. Stacy's poem had been more painful to write. I even put Stacy's name on the top so she wouldn't give it to Marsha.

STACY,
I AM A BOY IN YOUR SCHOOL,
WHO THINKS YOU'RE PRETTY
AND VERY COOL.
MEET ME WHEN THE CLOCK
STRIKES EIGHT.
I'LL BE THERE. DON'T BE LATE!

I lay back in bed and yawned. It was the best I could do. Marsha would be mad, but then she'd get over it. Nate and Stacy would have a wonderful time at the dance. I yawned again, hoping that a small tornado might pick me up and deposit me in the middle of Cleveland so I wouldn't have to go to the dance and watch any of it happen.

19

As soon as my alarm went off, I raced to the window crying, "Let there be snow!" No such luck. The sky was clear and snow free. February fourteenth. Happy Valentine's Day!

On the bus, I told Patrick I had the poems, but I didn't take them out of my backpack. Too risky. In the final stages of such a sneaky plan, I couldn't risk anyone seeing me holding the poems. In fact, I wasn't even going to take a chance by depositing them in the valentine boxes. I was going to make a special delivery right inside Marsha's and Stacy's desks as soon as possible, and then lie low.

Valentine's Day couldn't be over soon enough. I didn't want to see anyone today. Unfortunately, as soon as I got off the school bus, Nate Nelson wanted to see me.

"Hey, Roger, get over here," Nate called. He was standing over by the hedges, where the sixth graders hung out.

"Hi, Nate," I said. I stuck my hands in my pockets and nodded to his associates. "What's up, gentlemen?"

"That's what *I* want to know," said Nate. "Did you deliver the letter I asked you to?"

"I put it in her valentine box," I said truthfully. No need to burden Nate with unnecessary facts, like how a crazed girl named Marsha ended up with it.

"Roger," Nate whispered. "I just heard Stacy telling someone that she might not go to the dance. She said she might baby-sit." Nate scratched his head. "Are you sure you sent her the valentine?"

"Hey," I said. "I definitely put it in her box."

"Make sure she's at the dance."

I nodded, then checked my watch. "All right. In fact, I'll try to talk to her at our lockers in about five minutes."

Nate looked impressed. "Hey, you're all right, Roger."

"Thanks," I said quickly, turning to leave.

"I'll catch up with you at recess," he called as he raced across the yard. "Remember, tell her eight o'clock! Under the clock. Make sure she'll be there!"

I was almost to the front door when I felt a strong grip on my elbow. "Nate?" I cried, turning.

It was Marsha. She was puffing vigorously, as if she had just shoveled snow from New York to

Pittsburgh. The tip of her nose was bright red, and her eyes seemed to be sending sparks.

"Roger!" she cried.

I tried to free my arm, but her grip only tightened. "What do you want, Marsha? Let me go, my blood supply is being cut off."

Marsha released me, then even patted my arm. "Sorry, I just had to talk to you. It's very important." She glanced over her shoulder and then leaned closer. "Can we go someplace private?"

"Never!" I cried.

Marsha smiled. "I have to ask you something personal."

"Yes, I *did* shower today," I joked.

Marsha laughed. "I mean it, Roger. Can we talk for just a second?"

I was starting to feel uncomfortable. Marsha was actually acting like a normal girl.

"Okay. But hurry up, because I have to get something from the office." It wasn't a total lie. I thought I would use that excuse to get past the door monitor, then go into the office and get a peppermint from Miss Merkle, and finally slip down the hall and deliver my two poems, all before the school's front doors opened for business.

"I saw Nate," Marsha began. "Just now."

"Yeah, so . . ."

"So, I heard. I know." Marsha's nose twitched

slightly. Either she was about to sneeze or she was nervous. "So, now that I know, and . . . and I guess I'm . . ."

"About to sneeze?"

Marsha frowned. "No. I'm nervous now that I know about Nate."

I studied my shoes. What did Marsha know? Did she know that Nate liked Stacy?

"Nate is so popular, so . . ." Marsha sighed, and her nose nearly twitched itself off her face. "I heard him tell you to remind me about meeting under the clock at eight."

"What?" I sputtered.

"I was standing two feet away. Just now. I heard him talking to you. Tell him I will be there." Marsha smiled. "I can't *believe* he likes me."

"He doesn't even *know* you!" I cried.

Marsha patted my arm. "No need for any more secrets, Roger."

Marsha floated off then, almost evaporating into thin air.

I flew past the door monitor, mumbling something I couldn't even understand. A crowd of PTA mothers were clustered in the office with dance decorations, so I flew past Miss Merkle's desk and headed down for my homeroom.

Things were getting off track. In fact, the train was about to derail. I had to get the poems in the proper desks and then wait for everyone to know their places and stay there. Marsha would stay home, Stacy would be under the clock, and with any luck, I'd be able to hide comfortably under my bed until the clock chimed midnight. If I made it to February fifteenth, I would be okay.

20

Mrs. Pompalini was writing at her desk when I skidded into the room.

"Why, Roger. Good morning," she said cheerfully.

"Happy Valentine's Day," I said quickly. Right away I felt bad that I didn't bring her a box of candy. My mother had one on the kitchen table, but I refused it. I mean, I love Mrs. Pompalini, but I just felt too *old* to give my teacher a valentine present this year. Maybe because it was the first year I wanted to give a girl a present.

"Did you want to see me about something?" asked Mrs. Pompalini. She closed her lesson plan book to let me know I was more important than her work.

"Well." I tried to think clearly. There was probably some sort of rule saying that no kid was allowed in the building before first bell, *unless* that kid had a serious need for a talk with his teacher. I looked up. Mrs. Pompalini had both eyebrows raised, like she was actually hoping I wanted to discuss something.

"Yes, actually, I did want to see you," I began. I edged another foot into the room, in case Sister Mary Elizabeth had turned on her radar and was trying to check the halls for short people who should have been outside waiting in the cold.

Mrs. Pompalini waved me over. "I'm glad you came in, Roger. Now, tell me what's on your mind."

I almost cracked and told her the whole awful mess. It was so tempting. Maybe Mrs. Pompalini could talk to Stacy and Marsha privately and tell one to stay home and the other to dress up and stand under the clock. She could promise them both an A in conduct for agreeing.

"Roger?" Mrs. Pompalini was staring at me with a worried look, as if I had been talking to myself. Maybe I had been.

"I . . . I guess I wanted to ask you if I could deliver two valentines ahead of homeroom period. Before all the other kids came in." I patted my backpack. "I'm new to this sort of thing and I . . . I guess I didn't want a crowd."

Mrs. Pompalini sprang from her chair. For a wild second, I thought she was going to hug me. "Oh, Roger, that is just so candid and delightful." She picked up her coffee cup and hurried to the door. "As a matter of fact, I was just on my way to have one quick cup before the bell rings. You take your time, dear."

She sailed past me, cup in hand. I smiled, inside feeling like a dirty liar. But I wasn't lying, not really. I *did* have two valentines to deliver. But . . . my head pounded. The trouble with lying was that anyone could make it sound like the truth if they had a way with words like I did. Knowing how to use words was a talent. Lately, the only way I had been using my talent was to keep a step ahead of trouble.

I got out the poems and reread each one. I double-checked to make sure Stacy got the right one. I slipped it into her desk. I walked over and picked up the lid of Marsha's desk. I started to chuck the poem inside, but my hand froze. Inside Marsha's desk was a tiny satin pillow. And pinned to the center was the original valentine I sent Stacy.

"Whoa," I whispered. That valentine meant so much to Marsha.

You hear people talking about something spooking them so badly their blood runs cold? Well, I shivered about ten times. It was like someone had poured a zillion gallons of slush down my throat. Without meaning to, I had convinced Marsha that some boy liked her. How was I to know that she wanted a boy to like her, almost as much as . . . almost as much as I wanted Stacy to like me.

It felt weird to think Marsha and I both actually wanted the same kind of thing. If I gave Marsha the exit poem, she would feel dumped. Which, technically, she would be. But since Marsha had such a gigantic mouth, the whole world already knew that she was to meet some kid under the clock at eight.

A bell rang and I jumped. For a second I expected a clap of thunder followed by a herd of angels riding in on horseback. Then I heard kids laughing and lockers slamming and knew it had been only first bell.

My gut reaction was to undo as much of what I had done as quickly as possible. I stuck Marsha's poem back in my pocket and raced over and grabbed the poem I had just delivered to Stacy and shoved that in my pocket, too. While I was trying to decide what to do with them, Mrs. Pompalini hurried back into the room. "Ready or not!" she laughed.

I tried to laugh, but it came out more of a squeak. Valentine's Day was getting closer and closer. At the rate things were going, I'd *never* be ready.

21

I'm not real proud of it, but ten minutes before lunch, I took the coward's way out. I raised my hand and told Mrs. Pompalini I had to throw up.

"That will teach you to look in the mirror," muttered Marsha.

I let the comment pass, since I had ruined Marsha's life.

"Oh, Roger, dear," cried Mrs. Pompalini, pushing her science book aside. "Come with me. Patrick, be in charge of the room for a few minutes while I accompany Roger to the nurse."

Another ton of guilt was dumped on my head when Mrs. Pompalini put her hand on my shoulder and tried to make me feel better. "Maybe you're just a little nervous about Valentine's Day, Roger. And there's nothing to be ashamed about. Why, I remember being so nervous the night of my junior prom, I asked my mother if she would call and cancel my date. Half my neighbors were standing on the sidewalk to get a look at my dress."

"Did you go?" I asked.

"Yes, and things were fine. So you relax and go to the dance tonight," Mrs. Pompalini suggested. "I'm sure you will have a good time once you get there."

I nodded and allowed myself to be turned over to the nurse. Nurse Adair glared at me. She wasn't an easy person to fool. I didn't have a fever, but even a suspicious nurse knows a green face is not a good sign.

Nurse Adair put in a call to Gram. I was being sent home.

"Oh, Roger!" Gram cried as she hurried me down the steps to the car. "Are you okay?"

"I'm okay, Gram." I sank into the front seat of the car, wondering if Gram would mind dropping me off at the turnpike. I could be in Ohio in less than two hours.

How could I go to the dance? How could I ever return to Sacred Heart Elementary? I hadn't fixed the Stacy situation. I hadn't removed Marsha from under the clock. I hadn't *done* anything except realize I couldn't *do* anything.

Last week I thought Valentine's Day was dumb. Now I knew it was *dangerous*. I was waaaaaaaaaaaay out of my league. The dance would be starting in less than seven hours. Nate and Marsha would go to the dance hoping to find their *perfect* valentines waiting for them, and instead would come home thinking this was the *worst* Valentine's Day ever. All because of me.

"Here, honey. I brought you a baggie, in case you have to throw up," Gram said.

I glanced down at the small baggie and started to laugh.

Gram laughed, too. "Well, let's hope you don't need it. In fact, you are looking better already. Now, is there anything you'd like before we go home?"

Yeah, can you find me a one-way ticket to Asia?

"Gram, I . . ." I zipped and unzipped the baggie. I felt weighed down, locked inside some moral trash compactor. Unless I coughed up the truth, someone was going to flip the switch.

"What is it?" asked Gram. She put the blinker on and turned onto Portland Avenue.

"I kind of lied a little."

Gram turned, raising both eyebrows. "Well, that's quite a trick, isn't it?"

"I didn't know that this lie was going to end up being so important." I closed my eyes for a second, wondering if I should just throw up so I wouldn't have to finish.

"It's okay, Roger," Gram said quietly. "Is there something I can do?"

"A sixth grader named Nate asked me to write a poem for his girlfriend. I did—but Marsha from Mars got it instead, and now the wrong person will be standing under the clock at the dance." I exhaled, feeling lighter already.

"I see," said Gram, pulling slowly into the driveway. "Well, it seems you've gotten yourself tangled up, haven't you?"

"Yes."

"Remember last Thanksgiving when I was knitting that sweater for your father, and your dog raced through the room and took my yarn with him?"

"Yeah." What did this have to do with me lying?

"Well, by the time we caught Leaks and got my yarn back, the tangle was so big I could barely carry it. And I remember thinking, 'Oh, pshaw! I might as well just cut this out and pick up with a new strand of yarn.' "

"Is that what you did?"

Gram laughed out loud. "Heavens, no. I paid good money for that yarn. I just figured it would take a little time and careful picking, that's all. So I started at one end of the tangle, and I just kept right on going till I ended up at the other end." Gram opened the car door. "Let's go inside, and you can rest."

I got out slowly, feeling better with each step. I didn't have a plan yet, but I wasn't as worried as before. All I had to do was find the end of the tangle and work from there.

22

I was still knee-deep in tangle at five-thirty. Gram tiptoed into my room, where I was pretending to sleep, and hung up my favorite plaid shirt.

"For the dance," she whispered, letting me know that she knew I wasn't asleep. On the way out, she slowly opened my curtains, letting the last bit of sunlight back in. "Got to get your vitamin D."

I sighed and tossed back the covers. Gram was right. I had to get out of bed and go to that dance and face the music. All of it.

I walked into my parents' room and pulled the phone book out from the nightstand. Once I called Nate and told him the truth, I would feel better, or at least know that he was on his way over to rip off my face.

"Nate, hi, this is Roger."

"Who?"

"Roger Friday, from school."

Nate laughed. "Oh, yeah. Sorry. What's up? I looked for you at lunch."

"I got sick. Suddenly." I coughed weakly.

"Oh. Well, did you have a chance to talk to Stacy before you left school?"

"No. But I was going to call her next. Nate, I have to tell you something."

"Okay."

"There was a slight mix-up with your valentine. It happens all the time in the postal system."

"What kind of mix-up?" asked Nate. He sounded bigger than ever.

"Well, Stacy didn't get the card. I mean, I put it in *her* box, but she gave it to Marsha."

"What? Who's Marsha?"

I drew in a deep breath. Marsha would have to be portrayed as a nice girl, or I could never get past the next tangle.

"Who's Marsha?" Nate asked again.

"She's a girl in my class. She has brown or black hair, nice teeth, really nice teeth, and . . ." I searched my mind for another good item about Marsha I could add. "She's in good health." I decided not to mention the mole on her nose.

"What are you talking about?" sputtered Nate. "Why'd Stacy give Marcie my card?"

"*Marsha,*" I corrected quietly. "Marsha Cessano."

Nate was quiet on the other end. Finally he spoke. He sounded confused, and a little scared.

"Hey, wait a minute. Is Marsha Cessano that girl who bounced a rubber spider off an eighth grader's head a few weeks ago? The girl who talks a mile a minute and is always pulling at her hair?"

The same Marsha.

"I know she likes to talk, and maybe she did bounce the spider. But she thought it was real, and she kind of overreacted, and . . ."

"That girl is nuts!" cried Nate. "What's she doing with my card?"

"Planning to meet you under the clock," I replied.

"No way," muttered Nate. "You messed up *big time*, Roger. I'm not meeting her."

"Well." I drew in another deep breath. "I thought if you danced with Marsha once or twice . . ."

"No," snapped Nate.

"Then I would make sure Stacy goes to the dance, and you could dance forty-five dances with her. Dance so much you won't even remember the two measly dances you had with Marsha."

"I can't believe this," muttered Nate. "I want my three bucks back, Friday."

"Sure," I said cheerfully. "So you'll do it?"

"I didn't say that."

"*Please*," I said. I wrapped the phone cord around my wrist. "I'll throw in an extra fifty cents. I heard you're saving money for the baseball card show. They may have a Nolan Ryan card."

"Yeah, well . . ." Suddenly, Nate laughed. "Hey, I heard *you* have a Nolan Ryan card."

I sat up straighter. Sure I had it. It was sealed in plastic, on my desk. It was my *best* card.

"Yes," I said, cringing with what was coming next.

"Okay, here's the deal. I'll dance with Wild Woman for the card."

My mouth fell open.

"Okay?" Nate asked.

It wasn't a bit okay, but since I was still so tangled up, I was in no position to say no.

"I'll bring the card to the dance tonight."

"And, Roger, one more thing."

"What?" Did Nate want me to bring my mom's silver tea service to the dance?

"Call Stacy for me. Get her to the dance."

"I'll try."

Nate laughed. "Boy, this is my lucky day. A Nolan Ryan card and Stacy Trinidad. Nice doing business with you, Rog."

"Yeah," I said softly as I hung up the phone. "Nice doing business with you."

I picked up the phone again to make my second call. Maybe I should get out the Yellow Pages, get myself a good attorney, and find a way to get Valentine's Day outlawed.

23

"**H**ello, may I please speak to Stacy?" I asked. "Why no, she isn't here, dear," said the lady.

I groaned. Stacy was already baby-sitting. Gone!

"Oh, just a second. I think I hear her now."

I smiled into the phone. "Thank you very much."

"Hello?"

"Stacy, hi. This is Roger Friday from school."

Stacy laughed. "Hello, Roger. How are you feeling?"

"Fine. It was . . . was just a two-hour flu. Weak germs. Strong me."

Stacy laughed again. "You are so funny, Roger."

"So, are you going to the dance tonight? Don't baby-sit, Stacy, it's bad for your health. Little kids are covered with germs and chocolate at all times."

"How did you know I was baby-sitting?" Stacy asked.

Yikes! How did I know that? I had been telling so many lies lately, I wasn't sure what was fact or what was fiction. Who told me?

"Anyway, my aunt doesn't need me to baby-sit anymore," said Stacy. "But I think you're real nice to want me to go to the dance."

"You do?" I yelped. I cleared my throat. "I mean, thank you, Stacy. I . . . I . . ." Here was my chance. I could just blurt out, "I like you more than any girl in the whole world." I could do it. Yes, I could.

"Stacy, I . . ."

"In fact, Roger," Stacy said, "you remind me so much of my little brother, Johnny, it's spooky."

"What?"

"He's almost six, and he's the funniest little guy you ever did see. He keeps us in stitches all the time."

My eyes narrowed. Little guy? *Six?*

"Roger?"

"What?" I snapped.

"Why, Rog, I . . ." Stacy stammered. "I hope you aren't offended that I said that. I mean, I just think Johnny is . . ."

"I know, funny, *little*, and six years old."

Stacy giggled.

"Listen, Stacy," I began. Suddenly I was all business. I had no life at this point, and I just wanted to clean up a few details and then go watch television with Gram. "A certain boy at school likes you and wants you to show up at the dance. In fact, show up and stand under the clock at eight. No . . ." I checked my watch. "Make that eight-fifteen. That's it. Will you do it?"

"I . . . I guess so," said Stacy. "But . . ."

"Great," I said, cutting her off. I didn't even know Stacy had a shrimpy little brother who made her laugh. No wonder Stacy thought I was funny. I reminded her of someone who still watched Bert and Ernie.

"See you tonight," said Stacy cheerfully.

"I doubt it," I mumbled as I hung up. There, I had done it. Organized the Marsha-Nate encounter and got Stacy Trinidad locked into place. That nasty ball of yarn was completely untangled. I was officially off the hook.

I sat back down, exhausted. If I had really accomplished so much, why did I feel so lousy?

24

I got to the dance so early, I had to wait outside with Miss Merkle, who had just arrived with the ingredients for the punch. At seven-ten, Mr. Doyle arrived and unlocked the door.

"You sure are early, Roger," said Miss Merkle. She was wearing a bright red dress and a white bow in her hair.

"I thought you might need some help," I said, picking up two of the grocery bags.

Miss Merkle smiled. "I sure wish there were boys like you around forty years ago." She picked up the glass punch bowl. "This is going to be so much fun."

I nodded, following her and Mr. Doyle into the school. As I passed under the clock, I said a quick prayer. I could hardly wait for eight-fifteen. By then the dust of the whole dance would have settled. I had already asked Gram to pick me up at eight-thirty.

"Thank you for setting up the table, Mr. Doyle," said Miss Merkle. "My, don't the decorations look pretty?"

The gym did look nice. Just then the doors opened again and Lenny Robinson, the local disk jockey, came in wheeling his equipment.

"Need any help?" I asked.

"Sure, young fellow," laughed Lenny.

I glared at him. I wasn't young. I was as far away from six years old as a fifth grader could get.

By the time I had helped Lenny, Miss Merkle, and a PTA mom I didn't even know, the doors were unlocked and the kids streamed in. Miss Merkle stamped my hand, shaking her head at my dollar.

"Can't take money from someone who is such a help," she said.

I shoved the dollar back into my pocket. If Marsha arrived at the dance looking too weird, I would probably have to throw it into the bribery pot.

"Hi."

I looked up, smiled, and stood up straighter. Then I fell back against the wall.

"Marsha?"

She grinned. "You didn't recognize me right away, did you?"

I blinked. No, I hadn't. Marsha's hair was straight and shiny, and she was wearing a dress that made her look like an eighth grader. And she was wearing perfume. Both Band-Aids were gone from her nose.

"How do I look?" Marsha bit her lip, then frowned. "Yuck, this lip gloss tastes gross." She wiped it off with her fingers, and then rubbed her hands together. "Tell me the truth, Roger. I picked you because you are basically rude and would tell me honestly."

"You look fine," I said. Actually, she looked great. Maybe I would be able to keep my dollar after all.

"Thanks." Marsha wiped her hands on the side of her dress. "I think I'm going to throw up."

"That will teach you to look in the mirror," I said.

Marsha grinned, then sighed again. "It's already seven-forty-two. Are you sure I look okay?"

"Sure, just don't talk."

Marsha swatted my arm. She was wearing pale pink nail polish. "Have you seen him yet?"

I looked across the crowd. Most of the kids were standing by the punch bowl, or shoving each other to get closer to Lenny Robinson's music table. I didn't see any blond hair sticking three feet above the crowd. Actually, I had to find Nate myself. I wanted to slip him the card before eight o'clock.

"There he is!" cried Marsha. She reached up to

tug at her bangs, then groaned and raced into the girls' room.

I hurried over to the front doors. Nate and his friends got their hands stamped, and then came over to me.

"I'll see you guys later," said Nate. His friends went into the gym.

"Is she here?" asked Nate.

"Yeah, she just raced into the girls' room. She's nervous about meeting you under the clock."

Nate grinned and slapped me on the shoulder. "Great. You told her about me and she canceled her baby-sitting job?"

"No, not Stacy. I mean Marsha is here."

"What about Stacy?" asked Nate. He peered into the gym.

I felt kind of bad for Marsha then. She was a nervous wreck pacing back and forth inside the girls' room, and Nate didn't even care.

I reached in my pocket and handed Nate the three bucks and my Nolan Ryan card. "Here you go."

Nate smiled. "Hey, cool. Thanks. Now, what time am I to dance with . . . Marcie?"

"Marsha!" I said loudly.

Nate laughed. "Hey, settle down, Roger. Marsha, Marsha, okay."

"Eight o'clock, right under the clock by the water fountain. Dance with her twice, and . . ."

"Once," said Nate. "I have to meet Stacy at eight-fifteen, remember?"

Before I could argue, Marsha came out of the rest room and Stacy and two of her friends hurried down the hall. Marsha turned and raced back into the rest room, and Stacy waited in line to get her hand stamped.

Stacy looked pretty. Okay, she looked more than pretty. Nate was staring at her like she was a movie star.

"Man," Nate said softly before he raced into the boys' room.

"Hi, Rog," said Stacy as she walked past. "You better save me a dance."

Stacy's friends laughed. Maybe Stacy had told them how much I reminded her of her baby brother.

"What's wrong with you?"

Patrick was standing in front of me. He was wearing a red tie.

I leaned closer. "Are you wearing after-shave?"

Patrick's face got as red as his tie. "I . . . my mother did it as a joke. It's got some sort of sunscreen in it."

I laughed. "Good, because the sun's rays are pretty dangerous at eight o'clock, Patrick. In the dark gym."

Eight o'clock! I stood back and checked the time. In exactly five minutes, I would find out if all my planning had worked. I knew now how the space shuttle scientists felt when the countdown began.

"Five, four, three . . ." I muttered.

"Are you all right, Roger?" Patrick asked again.

I nodded, not taking my eyes off the clock. In another four minutes I'd better be.

25

I wedged myself between the water fountain and the supply closet, my eyes never leaving the clock. At exactly one minute before eight, Marsha flew out of the girls' room as if shot from a cannon. She looked scared, shoving her bangs up with both hands.

"Don't touch the hair!" I hissed. For once in her life, Marsha was looking pretty good. She didn't have Stacy's dimples, or a normal personality, but Marsha looked great tonight. Almost human.

The electric clock at Sacred Heart doesn't have chimes, but at exactly eight o'clock Nate walked out of the gym. He didn't look a bit nervous. In fact, he looked very, very bored.

"Smile!" I wanted to shout. I had traded my Nolan Ryan for the dance, a smile should come with it.

"Hi. I mean, hi," said Marsha.

"Hi," said Nate. He smiled then. I felt better.

"So . . ." said Marsha.

"Yeah," Nate agreed. "We better dance."

I thought I was going to throw up. I bent down and started to drink. Any minute now something would go wrong. Nate would tell Marsha I had bribed him with a baseball card, Marsha would slap him, and then both of them would come after me.

By the time I came up for air, Marsha and Nate were gone. I leaned against the wall, then slid to the floor. I closed my eyes and sat there listening to the music. Gram would be coming for me soon. I could hardly wait. Wanting to spend time with a seventy-four-year-old grandmother seemed so great. So safe . . . so . . .

"So, Roger. What are you doing on the floor?"

I looked up into Stacy's dimples.

"Resting."

Stacy held out a hand and pulled me up. "You are so funny, Roger. Why aren't you inside dancing? The song's almost over."

I shrugged. "I was waiting for my grandmother. She's picking me up soon."

"You're leaving?"

"Well, I came early, so this is pretty late for me."

"But you asked me to come tonight," said Stacy.

"Yeah?"

"So."

"So." Stacy's face was getting pinker and pinker. She looked upset about something.

"But it's almost *eight-fifteen*," Stacy said.

I nodded, then froze! Stacy thought *I* was meeting her under the clock at eight-fifteen. And she seemed disappointed that I wasn't going to be there. I smiled, then started to laugh.

Stacy wasn't smiling.

Before I could answer, Nate and Marsha came back out into the hall. Marsha was limping, and Nate was pulling her like a red wagon.

"I'm sorry about stepping on you like that," said Nate. "I'll go see if I can scoop out some ice from the punch bowl."

"I'll be fine," said Marsha. "Now that your foot is off mine."

I laughed.

Nate got a bucket from the supply closet and turned it upside down for Marsha. "Sit here. I'll be right back."

Marsha waved her hand. "No, really. I'm fine. You go dance."

"No way!" Nate laughed. "I want to talk to you some more. Man, I never met a girl who knew so much about baseball. I can't believe you know so much about Nolan Ryan."

Marsha smiled. "He's my favorite. I felt so bad about his arm injury."

I blinked. Marsha knew baseball? She bragged about her parents having box seats for all home Pirate games, but I never thought she actually watched the game.

"I'll be right back," Nate repeated. "I want to talk to you some more."

I smiled, then frowned. Wait a minute. Nate was supposed to be meeting Stacy in a few minutes. There wasn't room under the clock for the whole school!

"I . . ." Marsha pushed up her bangs. "I'm fine. You go dance."

Nate laughed. "No way. I'm not going anywhere."

"Roger! Just the guy I wanted to see!" Marsha shouted.

Marsha! Just the girl I *never* wanted to see!

"Marsha, are you okay?" asked Stacy. "Can I get you anything?"

"Ice!" cried Marsha. "Go with Nate and get me tons of it."

Stacy smiled at Nate. "Hi. I'm Stacy."

Nate smiled. "I know. I'm Nate. I've seen you around school."

"I'll be okay. Roger will be here," Marsha insisted.

Stacy and Nate walked down the hall, and Marsha grabbed me and squeezed my wrist so tightly I expected my thumb to shoot off into orbit.

"Don't leave me," Marsha gasped.

"What are you talking about?" Her fingers were now Super Glued to my wrist. "I thought you'd be in heaven with your mystery man."

"The only mystery is why I thought he was so

wonderful." Marsha leaned toward me. "Sure he's the cutest kid in the school, has more friends than anyone, and is the star of the basketball team . . ."

"He sounds just like me."

Marsha grinned. "In your dreams, Friday."

"So what's the problem?" I asked.

"I'm not sure. The something I thought was there, isn't there."

"Where is it? The lost and found?"

Marsha smiled. "I don't know. And I'm exhausted, trying to . . ."

"Act normal? It must be a real strain for you."

She giggled. "It's just that Nate is so cute, so handsome, so popular, and . . ."

"Normal?"

"But he's just not funny," she said softly.

"Like me." I paused, waiting for Marsha to toss in an insult or two.

"Yeah," was all she said.

Nate and Stacy were walking down the hall, carrying a small bowl of ice. I glanced up at the clock. Eight-fourteen. Now what was I supposed to do?

"Marsha!" Nate called from the hall.

Marsha grabbed my hand and began dragging me into the gym.

"Roger!" Stacy shouted.

"Hey," cried Nate. "Wait up."

Marsha picked up speed, shoving me into the

center of the gym. "If Nate comes over here, act like you like me."

"But I don't," I wanted to shout. "I like Stacy and I'm about to find out if she likes me."

"Please, Roger," whispered Marsha. Her grip tightened. *"Please."*

Maybe it was because Marsha said please or because the whole valentine mix-up was my fault. The next thing I knew, I was dragging Marsha onto the dance floor.

"See you later," I called to Stacy and Nate. "They're playing our song."

"Our *song*?" groaned Marsha. "You didn't have to go overboard."

"It was a joke!" I said. "Can I help it if I'm funny?"

"Yeah, you sure are."

Marsha reached in her pocket and handed me my Nolan Ryan card. "Here, you can have this."

"Back?" My face was burning. Had Nate spilled the beans?

"Nate gave it to me. He said I knew more about the game than he did. Which is true."

I slid the card into my back pocket. "Thanks, Marsha. Are you sure you don't want it? To remember your mystery-man valentine?"

Marsha lifted up her foot. "I already have a reminder. It's called a broken toe."

I laughed. "Thanks for the card." It felt great to have my Nolan Ryan card back.

"Besides, I already have a rookie Nolan Ryan card."

"You do?"

"Signed." Marsha grinned. "Of course."

The music ended and another song started right away. It was a fast song, and lots of kids raced out onto the floor. I saw Nate and Stacy talking to each other by the bleachers. They didn't notice me.

"Well, I'm finished," said Marsha. "I'm going to call my mom and see if she can pick me up."

"My Gram is coming in a few minutes," I said. "She can drive you home."

Marsha called her mother to tell her, and then we both went outside to wait.

"Thanks again for the card," I said. The wind was beginning to blow harder and harder.

"It's okay. Maybe one day my dad can get it signed for you," Marsha offered. "My uncle's next-door neighbor knows Nolan Ryan."

"Wow!"

Neither one of us said anything for the next five minutes. We just got colder and colder. When Gram's car pulled up, I let Marsha sit up front, because of her smashed toe.

Gram talked most of the way home. But when Marsha got out of the car, she turned around and smiled.

"Thanks for the ride, Mrs. Friday," said Marsha.

"You're welcome, dear," said Gram. "Happy Valentine's Day. Roger, help your friend to the door."

"That's okay," Marsha quickly said. "I know the way."

"Your parents finally drew you that map, huh?" I said. I got out and walked alongside Marsha as she hopped her way to the front door.

"Well, guess I'll see you on Monday," I said. "Don't forget about the math quiz. You won't be able to count as well, now that your big toe is injured."

"Make sure you remember your crayons," Marsha shot back. "Especially the red one, for all your mistakes."

Marsha opened the door, then turned back to me. "Thanks anyway, Roger. For helping me escape from my valentine mystery man."

"Hey, Roger-the-Dodger at your service."

"Happy Valentine's Day! Thank goodness it only comes once a year," Marsha said.

"Just like your annual rabies shot."

"Roger!" Marsha started to slam the door, but I could hear her laughing.

I started laughing, too. Valentine's Day was over. Next year, I'd send Marsha a valentine card myself. If I started collecting now, there was no telling how many dead flies I could stuff in the envelope.

About the Author

Colleen O'Shaughnessy McKenna began writing as a child, when she sent off a script for the *Bonanza* television series. Ms. McKenna is best known for her Murphy books, the inspiration for which comes from her own family.

Valentine's Day Can Be Murder is Ms. McKenna's third book to feature Roger Friday and Marsha Cessano, two characters who first appeared in the Murphy books. Her other Roger and Marsha books are *Good Grief . . . Third Grade* and *Live From the Fifth Grade*.

In addition to the Murphy books and their spin-offs, Ms. McKenna has written *Merry Christmas, Miss McConnell!*, the young adult novel *The Brightest Light*, and original books based on the television series *Dr. Quinn, Medicine Woman*.

A former elementary-school teacher, Ms. McKenna lives in Pittsburgh, Pennsylvania, with her husband and four children.

.PPLE® PAPERBACKS

Pick an Apple and Polish Off Some Great Reading!

BEST-SELLING APPLE TITLES

❏ MT43944-8	**Afternoon of the Elves** Janet Taylor Lisle	**$2.99**
❏ MT41624-3	**The Captive** Joyce Hansen	**$3.50**
❏ MT43266-4	**Circle of Gold** Candy Dawson Boyd	**$3.50**
❏ MT44064-0	**Class President** Johanna Hurwitz	**$3.50**
❏ MT45436-6	**Cousins** Virginia Hamilton	**$3.50**
❏ MT43130-7	**The Forgotten Door** Alexander Key	**$2.95**
❏ MT44569-3	**Freedom Crossing** Margaret Goff Clark	**$3.50**
❏ MT42858-6	**Hot and Cold Summer** Johanna Hurwitz	**$3.50**
❏ MT25514-2	**The House on Cherry Street 2: The Horror**	
	Rodman Philbrick and Lynn Harnett	**$3.50**
❏ MT41708-8	**The Secret of NIMH** Robert C. O'Brien	**$3.99**
❏ MT42882-9	**Sixth Grade Sleepover** Eve Bunting	**$3.50**
❏ MT42537-4	**Snow Treasure** Marie McSwigan	**$3.50**
❏ MT42378-9	**Thank You, Jackie Robinson** Barbara Cohen	**$3.99**

Available wherever you buy books, or use this order form

Scholastic Inc., P.O. Box 7502, 2931 East McCarty Street, Jefferson City, MO 65102

ease send me the books I have checked above. I am enclosing $_____ (please add $2.00 to over shipping and handling). Send check or money order—no cash or C.O.D.s please.

Name_____Birthdate_____

ddress_____

ity_____State/Zip_____

ease allow four to six weeks for delivery. Offer good in U.S. only. Sorry mail orders are not ailable to residents of Canada. Prices subject to change.

APP596